A POET IN PITTSBURGH

DOROTHY NORTH

ISBN: 978-1-64184-535-9 (Paperback)
ISBN: 978-1-64184-536-6 (Ebook)

Table of Contents

CHAPTER ONE

What Happened

MY NAME IS DONNA, and my life was pretty ordinary until I made the mistake of getting into a car with John Smith. I feel embarrassed to say that this experience has defined my life, to a pretty big extent. But truthfully, it has. There isn't a day that goes by that I don't think about it. I don't really think about John that much, and I really don't know what his life is like now, in jail. But the way I think about him is the way he was in high school, a bullying, swaggering football god who nobody dared to challenge.

And in my mind, I challenge him every day. Either I'm in some imaginary court room, sentencing him, not for the actual murders he did commit, but for the small murders of other students' self-esteem and aspirations, back in the fifties when we were all in school together. Or I imagine kicking him in the fork, jumping out of that car, and picking up some heavy object and smashing that precious car's lights out, before running off into the night like a victorious Valkyrie. I imagine numerous outcomes that are the exact opposite of what actually did happen, because what happened resulted in the crashing demise of my future as a loving relationship partner and a happy, productive member of society.

Although I actually am productive, I continually have to remind myself of it. I wasn't crushed completely. I do make a contribution, and there are those who think I make a big contribution, but I am not among them. I do not tend to see my accomplishments in the same light as others do, and in fact, I am not sure I see them at all, much of the time. But the defeats weigh large in my mind. Still, I keep going. It never occurred to me not to. I am continually fascinated by life, and what fascinates me most is when people climb out of the gutter to remake themselves. I can't go back and change what happened that night, but I can help other people to avoid making similar mistakes, or to rise above their mistakes and claim the gifts their lives can potentially offer. As in the old saying, those who can't do, teach. And I am constantly amazed by the resilience of people. Working with homeless, addicted, sometimes mentally ill people gives me constant examples of that.

Back to what happened that night. It was sometime in the fall of our junior year of high school. My friend Denise got a car for her sixteenth birthday, and she got me and our friend Miranda to go with her to some drive-in hamburger place where kids from our school went to hang out and drink beer. It was after a big football game, and Denise had her eye on John Smith. God knows why, but she has always been one of those girls who likes mean guys. Meanwhile, he really liked Miranda, and she couldn't stand him. So, going to this place was never a great idea, but Denise and Miranda were crazy to go and get their hands on some beer. Both of them had recently discovered they really liked drinking. It didn't appeal to me that much, but they were my best friends, going back to grade school, so I went.

It was exciting, I have to admit, sitting at a picnic table surrounded by kids from our school, most of them older. John Smith was bragging about scoring a touchdown during the game that afternoon. He started to talk to Miranda, but she ignored him and walked away to talk to some other boy. He watched her go, expressionless, which I guess is how he looked when he didn't feel so good. Then he sat down across from me and Denise. "What am I doing wrong, that Miranda doesn't like me?" he asked us, "I keep trying, but nothing works."

"You aren't always Mr. Nice Guy, John," said Denise, "but that doesn't bother me. It was amazing when you tackled that guy and got the ball for the touchdown. So what if the guy got hurt, it wasn't your fault."

"I just hope I didn't put him in the hospital for too long," said John, with a sappy expression of fake humility on his face.

He always said that after football games, and I always hated it. I tried to think of something to say that hid how much I disliked the guy. I finally said, "Maybe she would talk to you if you tried being a little nicer to people when she was around."

Denise retorted, "Nah, forget it, it's a lost cause. If she won't go out with you, I will. Wait till I get my sweater," and she walked to her car to get it, swinging her hips.

I watched her go, feeling in my stomach that something wasn't right about this. I asked John Smith how he was doing, and he just grunted. Then he said, "You know, Donna, I really need to talk with you about Miranda. Could we go and talk in my car for a minute?"

This is where I should have got up and left. Instead, I said, "Shouldn't you wait for Denise? She likes you, you know."

"She's not really my type," he said, which was probably something he got from a movie, since who at age sixteen, or he might have been seventeen, has a "type," anyway.

Getting in the car was where I really went wrong. He didn't really want to talk about Miranda. He said he wanted to go somewhere more private, which I took to mean his house, but we wound up at the parking lot at the Lake, of all places, which was totally deserted. Suddenly he was on top of me and I couldn't breathe. I passed out for a while. After I came to, all I really remember is telling him over and over to get off me and take me home, and he kept ignoring me and doing more and more stuff I didn't want him to do. By the time he dropped me off it was the early hours of the morning, and I felt like some torture victim who suddenly got released.

All I wanted to do was get myself to my room, maybe get some coffee to try to calm down and stop shaking. But my older sister was up, watching some late-night movie, and when she saw me, she knew something was wrong. "What happened?" she asked, with a look in her eyes I didn't like.

"Nothing," I said, "I'm just going to get some coffee and go to bed. I don't want to talk about it."

I went to the kitchen and put some water on to boil. I stood by the kitchen counter, shaking and wondering if I was going to throw up. I wasn't even aware that my sister was in the room until she was standing right in front of me. When I looked up and saw her, I jumped a little and held on to the kitchen counter so I wouldn't lose my balance. "What do you want?" I asked her, with a tone like, *go away*.

Her eyes narrowed. "Where did you go? I thought you were just going out with your friends, but you look like something happened. Did you meet a boy, or something?"

"Like I said, I don't want to talk about it," and as I was talking, my voice began to quaver.

I sounded hysterical. I tried to control it, but I couldn't. She continued, "What happened? I'm guessing you went somewhere with some boy. I thought you were smarter than that."

I took a breath, and answered, "What happened is none of your business. Now I'm going to take this coffee to my room. I don't want to talk with you."

"Are you still a virgin?" she asked. I looked down, then tried to get calm so I could put some sugar in the coffee and leave.

"Oh, boy," she said, "you're not, are you? Something really happened, all right."

"It wasn't my fault," I managed to get out in a strangled tone, "now leave me alone."

"Wow," she said, "I didn't think you were stupid enough to let something like that happen. You better make sure Mom and Dad don't find out."

I had picked the coffee up, but now I thrust it down with a slam. "You leave me alone," I said.

"Dad might have another stroke," she jeered.

"That's it," I yelled, and picked up a small, sharp knife that was sitting on the counter. Probably my Mom had been using it to peel fruit, as she used to do. I held it in front of Karen, and yelled again, "I've had it."

She stared at me. "What do you think you're going to do with that? Stab me? Like hell you will," she said, trying to grab it.

I threw the knife in the sink and slapped her, hard. She stared at me and blinked back tears. I said, "Yeah, okay, I'm not going to stab you, but you better leave me alone or I will give you such a beating," finishing in a whisper and staring back, thinking where to hit her again. I don't know exactly how but my mind had gone white hot with rage, and it was making me do things I would never normally do. And I really felt like I could kill her, just to get her to leave me alone so I could go have my coffee in my room and try to stop shaking.

She must have picked up that I was serious, because she backed away from me, with fear in her eyes, and let me leave. As I went to my room she called out, "You better hope that boy doesn't tell everybody you know about this."

I just kept going until I got in my room, sat down on my nice, comfortable bed with the quilted pink bedspread and three teddy bears, and sobbed until I fell asleep.

CHAPTER TWO

The A&W

I DON'T REMEMBER MUCH about that Sunday. I spent most of it in my room, telling my parents I didn't feel well and avoiding my sister completely. The next day was Monday, and I was dreading going back to school, but I went, because how could I get out of it? In our house, you had to be bedridden with a fever of at least 101 degrees to stay home from school, and though I hated Karen right now, I thought she was right about not telling my parents what happened. So I went, but I knew it wasn't going to be good. John Smith was in my homeroom, and I didn't want to be anywhere near him, but I couldn't think of a reason not to go. I went, sat down as usual, and started looking through my purse, not for anything special, just for something to do. Then I took a book out and started reading. I heard noises from his direction that he was talking to another boy and laughing, and I knew it was probably about me, but I figured as long as I didn't look at them, I could just sit there and pretend nothing was going on. I could feel my face turning red, and I tried to will it to stop, but I don't think it worked.

My friend Denise came in and sat at the desk next to mine. As usual, the first thing she did after sitting down was to look around and see what was going on with John Smith. Sometimes she would just sort of turn her head half-way and glance at him from the side, but it was still pretty obvious what she was doing. Most days, I would just accept this as how it was with Denise, but on this day, for once, it made me angry. Seemed to me, she needed to know that John Smith was a piece of crap who couldn't care less about her, but I couldn't tell her that in homeroom. So, when she asked, "Do you know what those guys are laughing about?" I said, "I can't tell you now. I'll tell you about it at lunch."

Then I just tried to ignore her while she kept looking from me to him. Finally, she leaned over and said, "This is about Saturday night, isn't it? Miranda called and said she thought she saw you leave with him, but I said, that was impossible."

I wouldn't look at her. I just whispered again, "I'll tell you about it at lunch. Not now."

It surprised me that I got emotional all of a sudden; my voice choked up and I felt my face flush. It even felt like I might start crying, but I took a deep breath and managed to calm down a little. Fortunately, homeroom was ending, and everybody was getting up to leave. I heard Denise say, "Well, okay, I'll be looking for you."

Once I left the room, I was able to breathe better and I walked around the school for a few minutes, just to calm myself down. Lucky for me I didn't have any classes with Denise or John that morning. When I was calm enough to face my first class, I went in and just focused on my books. That was how I got through the morning, just doing that and getting through one class after another. Then on my way to the cafeteria for lunch, I saw Denise, and almost burst into tears. "Donna, what?" she said, when she got closer to me, "what is it? What could have gotten you so upset? I haven't seen you like this since your hamster died in third grade."

I said, "We have to go outside, I can't talk about it here."

We walked from the cafeteria to the gym and out the back door of the locker room. There weren't many kids around the playing fields just then so we found a place behind one of the bleachers where we could talk. Then I turned toward Denise, took another tissue out of my bag, and said, "Look. That guy John, he isn't…." I had to take a second to stifle a sob. "He isn't what you think. He's a really bad person. He acted like he needed my help, he wanted to talk about Miranda, I don't know … All I know for sure is, I shouldn't have got in that car with him. My sister told me I was stupid. And I was, I really was."

She put her arm around me and got out some more tissues from her purse. "Oh my God, Donna, you got in his car? What did he do?"

I had to take a minute to stop sobbing. I took a few of her tissues, wiped my face a little and went on. "He said we had to go somewhere quieter, I don't know. I guess I thought he meant his house or something, I didn't really think about it. We wound up by the lake, and all of a sudden he was on top of me, and he did … pretty much whatever you can think of.…"

I couldn't talk anymore. I kept crying, and then I managed to blow my nose again and look up at her. She was taller than me, a pretty brunette with high cheekbones and big brown eyes, kind of like a tall Audrey Hepburn, while I was like, well, maybe a chubby Doris Day.

Her expression at that moment was hard for me to describe. Pity mixed with anger, I suppose, with maybe a bit of what might almost be jealousy, but as I looked at her, she melted a bit, and gave me a hug. "Aw, you poor kid," she said, "I can't believe this happened to you. And I was ready to get in that car with him, that would have been me."

"He said," I got out between sobs, "he said you're not his type, whatever that means. Lucky you."

As I said that, we noticed a shadow crossing to the right of us, and as we turned and looked, blinking in the sun we saw that John Smith was there. He must have walked quietly to sneak up on us. I just gaped, my face wet with tears, and Denise was looking at him sharply and distastefully, like he was one of those formaldehyde frogs for science class. He said, "Well, I came out here to look for a football that I lost last week, and look who's here. Denise, I guess you know what happened, sorry I didn't have time for you, but I do now."

He had a mean sneer on his face and went to grab Denise's hand. I went into a rage that dwarfed what I had felt toward my sister the other day. "Don't you touch her, you . . . ."

"What, Donna? What are you going to do about it?" he said, with an especially ugly look on his face. Something took hold of me, and with a strength that I never had before, I took a step toward him and then forcefully planted my right foot into his crotch. I wish I could say I was wearing high heels, but those saddle shoes could still pack a wallop. He doubled over and vomited.

I backed up, exhaling with a small scream, my hands in front of my face, not believing what I had just done. I looked at Denise, and she looked back at me, just as scared and breathless as I was. We kept looking at each other, stunned, for almost a full minute, and then Denise whispered, "Donna, I think you better leave, now."

"Yes," I whispered back, and then I grabbed my purse and took off along the top of the football field as if I was running to make a goal, except in the wrong direction.

Beyond that were woods, with brambles that stuck and scratched my legs, but I didn't notice that till much later. After a few minutes there was a clearing, and I realized I was in someone's back yard. I skirted down the side of the yard to the driveway, thought about taking the road but I got this wild idea that John might go looking for me in his car. I kept going down the edge of people's backyards.

Finally, I made it to the main road, the one that went from the nearby college town on into

Possumtown and beyond. This was exactly where any-one might look for me if they wanted to. So I kept going, cutting down to another road further back but parallel to the main road, that went behind the store, and when that road had a dead end, I crossed to the other side of the main road and went along the back of people's back yards again. Fortunately, nobody seemed to notice, or at least that was the way it seemed to me. I was getting close to the road that went to my house, that right-angled the main road from the A&W. Before I got to that road, I had to cross a field, and I slowed down, because I didn't want to go home yet. My parents would ask questions, and when my sister got home, she might yell at me. I found a place in a field near the road to my house where there were some trees for cover and sat down, breathing heavily.

I took stock of the damage to my legs, socks and shoes from the brambles and branches that hit me as I ran. The saddle shoes only had a few scratches but were caked in mud about halfway up. I started slowly pulling burrs out of my socks, wondering what to do next. It was a chilly fall day, but I was wearing a jacket and the sun was warm on my face. I must have fallen asleep, because it seemed like the next thing I knew, it was beginning to get dark. The sun was low in the sky and I knew I had to get out of that field because it would be hard to find my feet in the dark. Also, my stomach was reminding me that I hadn't eaten lunch.

I staggered up, brushed myself off and went along the edge of the field, stealthily walking past my house on the opposite side of the road. I had thoughts of sneaking into the house, but my Mom was in the garden, so I headed down to the main road to the

A&W. I had just enough money in my purse to get a root-beer float. I bought it and went to sit in a corner, as far from the counter as I could get, in case anybody I knew came in. I got out my book and started reading, and I think maybe an hour or two went by before a shadow fell over my book and I looked up to see a policeman standing in front of me.

He was tallish, maybe just six feet, but skinny, and with a nice but forgettable face, kind of a squashy nose that looked like it had been broken, but with a very thoughtful expression, like he was visiting from another time and was keen to observe everything microscopically. He was maybe about ten years older than I was. I just looked at him, hoping he made a mistake and didn't really have anything to say to me. "Is your name Donna?" he asked, raising his eyebrows a little.

"Yes," I said, thinking to myself, *say as little as possible.*

"Your parents called the police station to ask for someone to look for you, and they sent me. That was just a few minutes ago. Lucky guess that I found you here. What happened, that you didn't go home?"

I just looked at him, again, thinking, *can I tell him about John Smith?* But then tears came to my eyes and I didn't think I could speak without crying, so I didn't. "Well, you don't have to tell me if you don't want to," he said, "but I would like to take you home, if that's all right with you. Your parents must be worried."

Just then the door to the A&W swung open and Karen stomped in, car keys in her hand. "Donna, you're here," she yelled, with a look of triumph, as if she'd won a competition. "I just got home a half an hour ago and Mom told me you weren't home and she was so worried. This is the first place I looked. I knew you'd be here. You love a root-beer float, don't you?"

Then she noticed the policeman and said more quietly, "Is there some problem, officer?"

"No," he said, laughing a little, "by coincidence, this is the first place I looked for her, too. Your parents called the police station only a short time ago. If you can show me some ID, I can let you take her home."

"Sure, officer," said Karen, batting her eyes ever so slightly. I looked from her to him. His face had gone to a fixed expression. Somehow, I was relieved that he wasn't interested in flirting with my sister. She showed him her driver's license and he said, "Sure, okay, that seems fine, you girls can go on home."

Karen hesitated. "Aren't you going to say something to her, like, 'Don't do it again?'" she asked him, batting her eyelashes again.

"She doesn't look like she skips that much school. In fact, she looks like she had a tough day. I hope you and your parents take it easy on her."

"Wow," Karen said, "you're not exactly Mr. Tough Guy, are you? You're awfully nice for a cop. Can we call you if we have any more problems?" She batted her eyes again.

"You can feel free to call the police station any time, ma'am. Have a good evening now," and he left, quickly, his face totally expressionless.

Karen laughed a little and turned to me. "So, what happened?" she said, and I was a little surprised to see that she was really concerned.

"I had to get away from the school," I said quietly. "I did something bad."

"What on earth could that be?" she said, laughing again, "Did you beat somebody up?"

Somehow, I got the feeling that it might be okay to tell her, so I said quietly, "John Smith was bothering me and Denise, so I kicked him."

"You kicked him?" Karen gasped, "Quiet little you? What, in his you-know-where?"

"Yeah," I said quietly.

She leaned her head back and laughed loud and long. I looked over at her, trying to gauge her reaction. Was she angry? She stopped to wipe her eyes and said, "Donna, wow, that is just amazing. I'm surprised he didn't beat you up, though."

"He couldn't," I said, "he was on the ground. He threw up, too."

She laughed again and looked at me, smiling admiringly, "You got him good, huh?"

I looked down and said, "You're not mad?"

"Mad?" she exclaimed, "God, no. I am proud of you. Finally, you did something that makes total sense to me. I am glad you got him real hard, too."

We got in her white VW bug and she started driving, still giggling and wiping her eyes again. "But we still can't tell Mom and Dad. They won't be able to deal with it, seriously."

I said, "I'm scared to go back to school."

"Oh," she said, "well, naturally. But don't be. I think it'll be all right. I know how these things go. I was popular in school, not like quiet little you. I'm pretty sure he won't want people to know that a girl beat him up. You should be all right, but if he gives you a problem, let me know. We could probably even get that cute cop to help us."

She laughed again and clapped my shoulder. "Kicked that mean boy right where it hurts. Good for you, kid."

"I'm glad you're not mad," I blurted out. "I thought you really hated me."

"Oh, because of the other night? Well, I can't imagine why you picked up that knife. I guess I didn't get how upset you were. I am kind of disappointed that you got into the car with that boy, but life goes on, I guess. Worse things have happened. And I wasn't happy to hear that you didn't make it home from school. You're a funny little thing, and I don't always get you, but I'm really glad I found you and that you're okay."

She pulled up to a stop in our driveway, in front of the big barn-like structure that Dad used as a garage. She looked at me, kind of serious and smiling a little. I thought she might hug me, but she just patted my shoulder and said, "Let's go find Mom and Dad and let them know you're all right. I think Mom has some meatloaf and mashed potatoes still warm for you."

"Oh, boy," I said.

••• CHAPTER THREE •••

How I Started Smoking

THE REST OF HIGH school went by pretty uneventfully for me. I still spent a lot of time with Denise, but not that much with Miranda, who was all wrapped up with her football player boyfriend. Sometimes, Denise would tag along with them to parties where there was drinking, but I didn't go. That kind of thing held no interest for me anymore. I liked to stay home with the radio on, reading books or watching TV. I loved watching the Red Skelton show with my Mom and Dad, and my sister and I both had crushes on Maverick.

Toward the end of my junior year, when the weather was warm, there was a big party at the house of some boy whose parents stupidly left him alone for the weekend. Denise begged me to go with her, but I stuck to my guns and stayed home, so I didn't know exactly how it happened, but she must have drunk a lot. She totaled her car on the way home, and her parents packed her off to stay with her aunt in Philadelphia. I missed her like crazy, and we talked on the phone a lot, but for the senior year of school I was mostly on my own. Of course, she found parties to go to out in Philadelphia too, and by spring she was back in Possumtown, with an auspicious bump on her abdomen. Miranda, coincidentally, had a bump also, and they were both obviously pregnant by the time we all graduated.

By that time, they were done with being embarrassed about it and used to joke around together at school. I felt a little left out, but relieved, in a way, that they were both okay and we were all still friends. But, unlike them, I had to plan what to do with my life. I finally decided that nursing school was a good way for me to go. A few of the girls in my class were going to study nursing at Penn State, which wasn't that far away, but I decided on Pittsburgh, I guess because I felt like I needed a change. The University of Pittsburgh had a good nursing program, and my grades were good, so I got accepted with no problem. My parents complained that it was a two-and-a-half-hour drive from home, but I told them I would be home most weekends, at least to start with, and they calmed down. I got the feeling they were proud of me, especially my Dad, who used to tell me how some nurse saved his life during World War Two.

Pittsburgh was so big, compared to Possumtown, that I was scared at first, but people at the school were mostly friendly and the staff tried to help us settle in. I was living in a dormitory, sharing a room, kind of like how college students do now, except back then there were a lot of rules. Most of the rules were about keeping track of where we were, especially at night. We had to be back by 11:00 p.m. on weekends, and no boys were allowed in the building, ever.

For me, that was fine, but my roommate, Elaine, was a girl who liked parties. It seemed pretty familiar to me, being friends with Elaine, after dealing with Denise and Miranda back in school, except I was living right next to Elaine and couldn't avoid her. She used to tell me, "Donna, you need to loosen up, get out, have a few drinks and maybe have some fun for a change."

She was going to bars sometimes, and she met some guy who was sort of a beatnik type, who took her to parties where they played folk music and read poetry. I enjoyed hearing about it but had no intention of going until one night, when she kept bugging me to go with her to her boyfriend's party. "He shares an apartment with two other guys in Oakland. I can't go by myself, it's too far, and he won't pick me up because he's busy getting ready. Please come with me, please pretty please."

I finally agreed to go. We took my car, and when we got there, her boyfriend greeted her by giving her a big hug. "Who's this pretty lady who came with you," he asked, looking at me.

She smiled up at him, her pretty brown eyes opened wide. "I told you about my roommate, Donna," she said, and pretended to hit him.

I gave him a little wave and smiled at both of them, too overwhelmed to say anything. It was my first party since I started nursing school, and I wasn't prepared for how noisy and crowded the apartment was. Forget finding a seat, finding a place to stand comfortably would be enough of a challenge, even though it was a big apartment, an entire floor of a large house. We walked into the kitchen, all the countertops covered with bottles of booze or open beer bottles, with an old gas stove next to the sink and a huge old-fashioned fridge with white enamel doors and an ancient, slightly rusted handle. It seemed to still work, as the beer inside was certainly cold. Elaine's boyfriend's name was Chuck, as I knew from the innumerable times she'd been talking about him, and he handed beers to each of us before attempting to forge a path for us to enter the next room, which appeared to be a living room. We followed close behind, but it was slow going and Chuck kept stopping to talk to people. When they were girls, I could see Elaine getting jealous. He wanted to show us the record player, but there was such a crowd around it, we could barely get through, and the music was almost inaudible over the din of at least 50 people talking at more or less the same time. "I wanted to play you my Harry Belafonte record," Chuck was saying to Elaine.

I couldn't imagine how she would be able to hear it. She piped up, "I like Connie Francis; I should've brought my record."

From the look on Chuck's face, it was probably just as well that she didn't. I looked around but couldn't see much, apart from the students who were immediately next to me. One of them pulled out a cigarette and started smoking it. I tried to edge my way toward an open window; fortunately there were plenty of those. Some man was standing in front of the nearest one, with his back to me. He turned around, and I gasped. If John Smith had a brother, this guy could be him, except that the guy had a full, dark beard. Of course, John grew one just like that later, but that was after he came back from his military service. But this guy at the party scared the crap out of me, and I backed away, causing someone behind me to drop their beer.

"Excuse me, I'm so sorry," I said to the guy behind me, another tall guy who looked like he could be a football player. I thought of getting a dishrag from the sink to clean up his beer, but it would be too hard to get back to the kitchen, so I went for the other exit, to the left, toward another room that was full of smoke. There were fewer people there, and I thought if I waited long enough I might be able to sit down. But the smoke was making me cough, and I caught another smell in the air that I didn't recognize. I looked back to see if I could retreat, but the big guy with the beard walked through the door behind me with a cigarette in his hand. It didn't look like a regular cigarette. He gave me a kind smile and said, "Hey, I didn't mean to scare you. Nice to run into you again. I wanted to try this baby out," he flourished the cigarette, twirling it like a baton, and added, "You want some?"

"I don't smoke," I said, wondering how quickly I could get away from this guy.

"This ain't no ordinary cigarette," he said, "You ever tried pot before? You should give it a try, this is good stuff."

"I guess I heard about it, but I've never seen it before," I said, hesitantly.

He lit it with a match and took a huge drag, exhaling a cloud of smoke that had that smell to it that I'd noticed before. He smiled at me and held it up to my lips. "Come on, just one puff. If you never tried this, you got a treat in store."

Well, I knew I should say no, but I'd watched Karen try smoking cigarettes, and I was curious. Maybe something in me was thinking it would help me get over being scared. I don't know exactly why, but I went ahead and took a drag, and immediately started coughing. My lungs felt like they were burning. "Hey," he said kindly, "don't worry, everyone does that their first time. Take a sip of your beer."

So, I did, and as I stopped coughing, I began to take stock of how I was feeling. I was very light-headed, a feeling I couldn't remember having before, and I was starting to enjoy it. The music, what I could hear of it, almost took shape in my head, with the voice of Mr. Belafonte becoming some kind of seraphic entity unto itself. "Wow," I said, "I never heard music like that before," and I smiled up at the man.

"My name's Jim, by the way," he smiled down at me, and I said, "I'm Donna."

"Well, Donna," he said, "take another hit, if you want. I think you won't get much of an effect from it from just one."

"Another, wow, I don't know," I said, laughing, and watched him take another pull on the cigarette, which I suppose should properly be called a joint.

I laughed again, but when he handed it back to me, I looked up at him, smiled, and yes, I went ahead and tried it again. I guess I was still curious. This time I didn't cough as much, but my throat was on fire, and that light feeling became almost palpable. I thought I could almost hear something like a gnat that was buzzing my ear.

Then, as I was looking at him, my mind took a different turn. Suddenly I was noticing every wiry hair on his face like they were strange and ominous-looking little plants. His voice faded to nothing as I stared at his Adam's apple moving and a little voice in my head was telling me I had been here before and did not want to be here ever again. Then I took another look at him and I honestly thought I saw John Smith looking back at me. Even though I knew it wasn't him, part of me was sure it was and that I had to get out of there as fast as possible. I broke into a cold sweat and started to gag. Then I said with a stiff smile, "Excuse me, I have to get some air," and he asked me if I was all right.

I said, "I just need to get outside, and I'll be okay."

He said, "Let me help you," and I was saying that no, I didn't need help, and it seemed to take an hour, but I finally made it to the kitchen and started scrambling for the door.

I was dimly aware of Elaine yelling, "Where are you going?"

I looked in her direction and said I needed air, and she retorted, "Well, you better come back, I'm gonna need a ride home."

Jim turned up right behind me and said something I couldn't hear. I felt like I would die if I stayed in that apartment for another minute. I finally staggered out and looked around in a daze. Where had I parked? Jim came up and put his hand on my shoulder. I shrugged him off and took a step back raising my hands, but when I saw the stricken look on his face, I tried to smile. "Look," I said, "it's not your fault, but I just don't feel good. Maybe I'm allergic to pot."

"Maybe I shouldn't have pushed you to have some. Sorry you're not having fun. Do you need help finding your car?"

"No," I said, even though I did. "I'll be fine."

I took several breaths, looking around, trying not to panic. Then I spotted my car and felt like God had smiled on me. I turned back to him and was able to smile and say, "It was nice meeting you."

He smiled back and laughed a little, saying, "I'm not sure I believe that, but hopefully we'll meet again under better circumstances. You know where your car is?"

"Yes," I said gratefully, and waved bye as I went toward it, seemingly floating, almost. I heard him call "bye," and as I got in the car I looked back at the building and saw him watching me get in. All of a sudden, he didn't look that much like John Smith anymore, and I had the impulse to jump out of the car and go talk to him again, but my legs just wouldn't let me get up, for some reason. It was like my body went on strike, telling me I had to leave.

Driving back to the dorm was quite an experience. Every time I stopped at a stop sign or traffic light, I felt like I was still moving, sometimes backwards. The lights took on bulbous, three dimensional forms that almost seemed to flow up and down. I realized it was the effect of the pot and stopped being scared after a few minutes, but I was still light-headed, and grateful to get back to the dorm. I quietly greeted the dorm monitor, a nice older lady with brown hair and glasses who looked at me over her book and smiled. I ran upstairs to my room and got in bed, shutting my eyes to strange visions of encroaching black plants that waved ferny tentacles at me, and Elaine walking home in a mist, calling my name, but I couldn't move to go help her. After some time, I woke with a start, and realized that I was almost back to normal again. I got out of bed and looked at a clock. It was almost midnight, and no sign of Elaine. I felt a little guilty, but didn't worry much, figuring that her boyfriend would bring her back soon. She had missed the 11:00 curfew, but that was nothing new. I left my room and walked down the hall to the bathroom. The building was quiet, since we were supposed to be in bed, but as I walked past a room shared by a few friends of mine, I could see a faint light from under their door. I knocked quietly, and after a minute, the door opened, and a girl silently beckoned me in. She closed the door quietly behind us. Two other girls were sitting on a bed, listening to a radio that was turned down low, just loud enough that I could hear it, and it sounded like Roy Orbison.

Another girl was sitting by an open window, smoking a cigarette. I walked over and asked her if I could have one, and that is when I started smoking. Not pot, though. Never again.

CHAPTER FOUR

Finding Penny

ELAINE DIDN'T COME BACK till 2:00 in the morning. She said, glaring at me for leaving without her, that her boyfriend wouldn't take her home till the party was over. By the end of the semester, she was pregnant and quitting school to have her baby. She said, "I'll come back to finish when the baby's older, there will be plenty of time," but we both knew she probably wouldn't. I felt sorry for her, but kind of jealous at the same time. When she got married that summer, I noticed Jim at the wedding. He was with someone, so we didn't talk long.

Without Elaine, the following year of school didn't have nearly as much fun and excitement. There was a lot of hard work, however, and I buckled down, spending Saturday nights at the dorm, poring over my books with a Coke and a few cigarettes. I got a practicum assignment at the ER of the University Medical Center, which was a real challenge. I was elated when I found out, because I had been hoping to be placed there, hearing that many students who got that assignment wound up with job offers. That was my goal, to get a job in the ER of the busiest hospital in the whole big city, but I quickly learned there was a price to pay for having such an exciting job. The first day I was there, a young boy of maybe ten "coded" after he was rushed to the ICU. I don't remember exactly what was wrong with him, just the shock of seeing a young person die.

I saw my share of horrible accidents, gunshot wounds, and you name it, but one experience almost made me quit on the spot. Two pretty young women, younger than I, came in with one supporting the other, whose face was contorted with pain. I went to them and asked what the problem was. "Something happened to her," the one who was supporting the other one said. "She's my friend, but I don't know how she got hurt. She'll have to tell you."

I got the wounded young lady into a wheelchair and noticed blood dripping heavily down both her legs under her dress. Her socks were red with blood, and she was whimpering. I told her it would be all right, and turned to ask her friend a question, but she was gone. So, I asked the young woman, "Can you tell me what happened?" and she just shook her head rapidly without looking at me.

"Well," I said, "I need to let the doctor know what the problem is. Do you mind if I try to look at what's causing the bleeding?"

Again, she didn't speak, just shook her head and turned her face away. I gingerly moved her skirt to see if one of her legs was wounded, but I could see that the blood was coming from farther up. "Are you pregnant?" I asked, gently, "or having cramps?"

Then I looked more closely, and I noticed she was not wearing underwear. If my eyes were telling the truth, there was something protruding from her vagina. I lifted her skirt a bit more to get some light on it and I could see something glinting that looked like broken glass. I gasped, and my stomach contracted. I was terrified for a moment that I would throw up in front of this poor girl, but the moment passed, and I said, "I'll get the doctor now. Don't be scared, he's going to take care of you, and I'll be back to see how you're doing."

I went for a doctor as fast as I could, and I blurted out the briefest description of what I saw. He came running and she was swept off to treatment. Once she was gone, I was hit with a feeling that hit me like a freight train.

With the image of that poor woman's wound in my mind, I felt a twisting in my abdomen, almost like something similar had happened to me. I wanted to find a bathroom and throw up, but instead I staggered outside and lit a cigarette, trying not to cry.

The sun warmed my face a bit, and after a few cigarettes I began to feel like I could go back in, so I did. The ER was so busy, I didn't have much time to think about what had happened, and that worked in my favor, this time. Hours went by, and I remembered that I said I would check on that girl. When I went to find her, I was told she was in a bed a few floors up, so I went up to just see how she was, thinking she might be sleeping.

And she was. I glanced in on her, and looked at her drawn little face. She looked a bit younger now, not more than eighteen, and looking at her chart I saw that she wouldn't be eighteen for another five months or so. Her blonde hair looked like wispy straw, and she frowned as she slept, probably from the pain that might be returning as the anesthesia from her procedure wore off. I checked with the nurse that was attending her, to make sure she got something to take for the pain as soon as she woke up. Half an hour later, I came back and walked in on that same nurse, who was giving her the medication with some water. "Thanks for remembering," I said to the nurse, who smiled and said, "Hey, that's my job," then to the girl she commented, "Here's your friend who came to check on you earlier. I'll be back later," and left.

"Hi," I said, maybe a bit too brightly, feeling a bit nervous to be talking to this young lady at last. She looked at me guardedly.

I went on, "I see from your chart, your name is Penelope. Mine is Donna."

She just looked at me, then turned her head and said quietly, "I go by Penny, mostly," and stared at the wall.

Then she looked at me, frowning, and asked, "Why did you come back to see me? I'm not going to tell you what happened. I don't even remember most of it, but if I did, I wouldn't tell you anyway."

I just looked at her, wondering what to say. Finally, I asked her, "Where are you from?"

She looked down, frowning, and after considering for a minute, she said, "My Mom and stepfather live in Canonsburg, about a half an hour drive from here. But I don't want to go back there."

"Why not?" I asked.

"I don't like my stepfather," she said, slowly, looking at the wall again.

"Okay," I said, "that sounds like a good reason. But don't you think it might be a good idea to at least call your Mom and let her know how you're doing?"

"I did that once," she said, tersely, "but she wasn't listening to me, so I didn't call her again."

"When was that?"

"About three months ago, when I first came here."

"Well," I said, "it wouldn't hurt to call again, but that's just my suggestion. You do what you want. Are you hungry? Lunch isn't for another hour or so, but I can get you some tea and crackers."

"Yes, that would be great," she said eagerly.

"Okay," I said, "just a minute."

I went and found her tea with milk and sugar and some of those packaged cheese crackers with peanut butter. Then I left her alone. I didn't want to seem like a nag, but it troubled me that she would probably be in danger once she left again, unless she had somewhere safe to go. I sent up a brief prayer for her to make a good decision, and then I went about my business. Then later that afternoon, I was coming to the end of my shift, and I felt like I needed to see her again before I left work. She had just polished off another snack, and looked up at me, beaming, almost not recognizable as the girl I had left frowning at the wall.

"Listen," she said, "I called my Mom, and guess what. She made my stepfather leave the house more than two months ago, not long after I talked with her the last time. Turned out she was listening to me, but she just didn't sound like it at the time. She's been trying to get the police to find me, but they weren't really doing much. She was so glad to hear from me, and she wants to come and get me, but her car's not working and she doesn't have money for the bus. She's going to see if she can borrow it and call me back."

"Wait a second," I said, "maybe I can help you with that. Do you know when you are leaving?"

"They said the doctor was coming to check on me soon, and I can leave after that. Pretty soon, I think."

"I'm finishing up my shift in a little while, too. Why don't you call your Mom and tell her not to worry about it, and I'll call the bus station and find out when the next bus is."

"Wow, you can do that? Okay, I'm going to call her right now."

By this time, it was about four in the afternoon. I called the bus station and found out there was a six o'clock bus to Canonsburg, for about five dollars, which I could cover without a problem. It took another hour to get Penelope discharged, so I think it was about five o'clock when we headed out to the bus station. But as soon as we left the building, Penelope stiffened and gasped for breath. "What is it?" I asked her, thinking she was in pain.

Then I noticed a tall, thin man of maybe thirty years, sallow with curly brown hair, approaching us from across the street with a mean look on his face, staring at her. "Penny, come here," he yelled.

She broke away from me to run off, but I grabbed her arm and yelled, "Back in, back in the hospital, come on."

I pulled her back inside and she came with me, both of us trying to run, but the man caught up and came in the hospital behind us. I pulled Penny into the ER and ran toward the nurses' desk with her. "Help, call the police," I was yelling as the man rapidly approached us and grabbed Penny's arm. She fell to the ground, wailing, and he was dragging her by the arm, yelling, "Get up."

I saw an empty gurney nearby and grabbed it, ramming it into the man, breaking his grip and wedging it between the two of them. I knelt down to Penny and tried to pull her back toward the desk, but the man roared and tried to jump over the gurney on top of us. Just then, a large arm grabbed him by the shoulder and pulled him off the gurney onto the ground. It was one of the orderlies, a big man I hadn't noticed before. "You're leaving," he yelled at the man, and pushed him all the way through the ER to the exit. I held Penny as she cried hysterically, and then I looked up at the nurses behind the desk. "I was trying to get her on her bus home, but I don't know how I can get her there now."

"I have an idea," said the head nurse, an older lady with white hair and a determined gleam in her eye. "Let's get her into a wheelchair."

So, we put Penny in a wheelchair, with a blanket in her lap, and pushed her to the back entrance where the ambulances pulled up. The nurse had a word with one of the drivers and then turned and winked at me. "Can she get up in the front with you and the driver?"

Penny saw the ambulance and looked stunned. "I'm going in that?" she asked me.

"I'll come, too," I said.

"Wow," she said, "this might work," and she got up and hugged the older nurse, adding, "I can't thank you enough."

"Go ahead and get in," said the nurse with a smile.

We did, and I told the driver, "We just need to get to the bus station before 6:00."

"Where are you going?" he asked, "Oh, Canonsburg? I can get you there in twenty minutes, maybe less. Hold on."

The House

THAT DAY THAT I met Penny was only matter of weeks before I first heard about the Catholic Worker House. The Catholic Worker Houses were started by Dorothy Day, back in the 1930's, to help people who were made homeless and destitute by the financial vagaries of the time, during the Great Depression. They gave shelter and food to homeless men and women who needed help getting on their feet, sometimes just temporarily, but many stayed for a long time. The Worker House in Pittsburgh was for men only, but there were shelters for women in other locations. I'm aware of one in New York City, but so far have never visited it.

I got to know about this place one day while I was working at the ER. A nice older man came in, looking kind of scruffy in a coat that was worn to threads at the wrists and had a few buttons missing, and he'd scared himself by going out for a drink after taking his psychiatric medication. "I honestly didn't mean to have a drink," he said, nervously, "and I know I can't drink with my meds. I just went into the bar to talk to someone, and he just handed me a drink and I started drinking it without even thinking about it. Then I started a second one, and that's when the room started moving around on its own, and I realized I'd made a mistake. Do I need to have my stomach pumped?"

"I don't think so, but let's ask the doctor to make sure," I said, and then asked, "Where are you currently living?" And he proceeded to tell me all about the Catholic Worker House.

"They took me in after I came here from out by Reading, where I used to live. I had no money, so I was sleeping on a park bench. That was fine until it started raining. I wandered into a church where they were giving out food, and the people there told me about the House. I went over there right away, and they said they had room for me, and I could stay. I love it there. It's run by Father Douglas, he's just a skinny old thing and doesn't talk much, but the men all listen to him and he's the kindest person I've ever met. 'Pete,' he said to me, cause that's my name, Pete, and he said, 'you can stay here as long as you want, you just need to stop shouting so much,' and he laughed, because I'm always quiet, you know, and people are always telling me to speak up. And the food is so good. The cook really knows what he's doing. You ought to come by and take a look some time. I don't think there are many places like it."

He didn't turn out to need his stomach pumped. Just sent back to that House, with a caution to avoid alcohol, since he was taking a mild tranquilizer. I noticed him again when he came back for a follow-up visit a week later. "I feel just great," he said, "as long as I stay away from alcohol. It's been a really good week. Father Douglas suggested that I try a meeting. Turns out, they have one right down the road from the House, I don't know how I never noticed before. I went to one already and I feel like I'm on the right track."

"I really don't know much about those meetings," I said, "but I am glad it's working out for you. You do look a lot better."

"You should come by there some time when they're fixing lunch. That cook is amazing, you would love the food."

"Well, I will try to do it soon. I'm pretty busy for the next few weeks, though."

"Too bad, because I might be away by then. I'm going back to Reading to see family pretty soon. I'll be back, though. It was nice to see you again," he waved and gave me a smile as he was leaving.

But I think it was more like another few years before I wound up going over there to take a look. I kept thinking I wouldn't bother and that they wouldn't want me there, since I wasn't Catholic anyway. But I was intrigued, and eventually, I went. I wanted to see this place where sad little men like Pete would get help in such a kind and humane way. That's how it sounded from his description, anyway, and I wasn't disappointed. The first person I met there was an older woman named Jenny. I walked in to a small, dusty room with a crucifix and calendar on the bare, wooden walls and a desk with a few chairs. She was sitting comfortably, typing something with a mug of tea next to her. She looked up at me and smiled.

"How nice to have a visitor," she exclaimed, "I was getting so bored writing those reports. What can I do for you, young lady?"

"Well, I'm an ER nurse, and I wanted to come and see the Catholic Worker House after hearing about it from a nice little older man at the hospital. It was some time ago. He was very thin, his name was Pete, I think? He made this place sound wonderful, it seemed like you were doing him so much good. Sorry to say, it took me quite a while to get around to coming out here. My work keeps me so busy."

"Were you looking for Pete? He's gone for the last week or so. Probably visiting his mother. He never tells us, but he often pops off for a few weeks at a time and comes back."

"You know, I was wondering," I said, "since there's a lot going on in the world right now, what with demonstrations, people getting killed like those poor young men in Mississippi, and mentally ill people getting sent out of hospitals to live in the streets. Do you find that you see more people looking for help in recent years?"

"Oh yes," said the woman. "It's lucky we have a large building. It used to be a Home for Foundlings, babies that were unwanted, called St. Rita's. I think Father Douglas told me once that the first Worker House here in Pittsburgh was in an empty storefront somewhere not far from here, in 1937, but we moved here only a year or so later. Dorothy Day was involved in starting it, so it's thanks to her, and some local priests, that Pittsburgh has a Catholic Worker House. More than twenty-five years have gone by, but the need has never been greater."

"I don't know much about Dorothy Day, but I remember reading something about this place a few years back. Didn't she come here and visit? Did you meet her? I remember reading somewhere that she was accused of communism, is that right?" I couldn't resist asking.

"She's been here a number of times. Yes, I've met her and she's wonderful. I don't know about communism. She just believes this great country should take care of its needy folk. Seems like a good idea to me."

"Well," I said, "I have to agree we need to do more for people like your Pete, and the way he talked about this place really appealed to me. I don't know why it took me so long to get around to coming over here. Can I take a look around?"

"I guess there's no reason why I can't show you around, for a few minutes. Most of the time, people don't come in that door this time of day. In a few hours, we may get deliveries from some of our donors, mostly restaurants and grocery stores that have left-over food. You should really meet Father Douglas, he is in charge and knows more about the home than I do, his office is right through here." She pointed to a door in the back wall of her office, to the left of her desk, and continued, "But he is out meeting with some potential new donors and the people who run the Salvation Army, who sometimes send folks here.

That is what he spends most of his time doing, when he isn't counseling the men or conducting Mass."

"Truthfully, I have never met a Catholic Priest before, since I was brought up Lutheran and never set foot in the Catholic church where I am from. I would love to meet him. But it would be fine if you want to show me around. Do you guys have volunteers working here?"

And that is how I became involved with the Pittsburgh Catholic Worker House. That first day I came to visit was around 1964, I guess, but the place hasn't changed much since then. I really liked it there, maybe because I had friends who were alcoholics who wouldn't listen to anything I had to say, and at the House, the men had voluntarily given up alcohol. In fact, it was House rules that nobody could drink or be drunk in the House, but there is rarely any problem with that. Unlike my high school friends, these men, for the most part, really wanted to stop drinking.

I was just a volunteer until recently, helping on weekends, which cut into my already almost nonexistent social life, but I didn't much care. As a nurse, I was asked to do checkups for the men who had medical conditions, but when there was time, I loved helping out with meals. I was there usually just one day on the weekend, or during the week if that was when I had time off. Yves, the cook, was a lot of fun to talk to. He's older than I am, in his fifties, from Jamaica with the accent to go with it, but his wife was a Pittsburgh native and that's how he wound up here. They had five children, and most of them had been to the House with him at some point. Nice young people, tall like him but quieter, and with the same big charming smile he had. I guess they were used to laughing, living with Yves. I still hadn't met the youngest, a girl of two, while the oldest was a boy who was in high school. Then there was a thirteen-year-old girl, and twin boys, age twelve. The youngest was an "afterthought," Yves sometimes called her, and he loved to bring photos of her to work, taken with his Polaroid camera. He had one on the fridge, stuck under a magnet that had the name of a local supermarket on it.

So, occasionally one of his older kids came with him, but usually it was just Yves and me. Preparing and cooking the food was only a small part of the work, since Yves did all the planning and much of the cooking anyway. More important was to hang around during the meal and see who was sitting by themselves that might need someone to talk to. I really enjoyed some of the conversations, even though it was clear that some of the men were not in full touch with reality. This could be annoying, when some of them tended to repeat the same delusional ideas over and over. I learned to be patient with this, since that was the only reaction that ever helped. But even the most annoying sometimes could touch my heart. One of the guys, a World War Two vet, had been a classics scholar before he went away to fight and then returned to attempt to drink away his shell-shock. After one of these lunch-time conversations, he showed up the next day with a carefully written homemade card, entirely in Latin. I have never been completely sure what it says, but I keep it on a shelf in my living room.

And yes, I had a living room, because I had found a nice little one-bedroom apartment in a building in town, not too far from the hospital. It was in Oakland, close to where that apartment was when I went to that party years ago. There was a nice park not far from my apartment and I liked to walk by it when I went to the grocery store. People in the building were friendly, but I didn't have a lot of time to talk. Between my job and my volunteer work, I really didn't have much free time. I didn't even get back to Possumtown all that often. I had wound up with Karen's VW bug around the time I went off to nursing school, and after she got married to a nice man that she'd kind of snubbed in high school, but I guess she finally decided he would do. He worked in town for the sanitation department. They had a daughter the year I graduated high school, my adorable niece Mandy, who wound up going to school with Denise and Miranda's kids, coincidentally. I was sad about being away in Pittsburgh while Mandy was growing up, but she was a happy baby and had no serious health issues. I felt that as long as all was well with Karen's young family and my parents, they didn't really need more from me than a few visits a month, or sometimes more around the holidays. So, I wasn't in Possumtown that much and didn't really see my friends much at all, until we had the five-year high school reunion, which was quite an experience. It will take me a while to describe it, but I think it's at least a good story and deserves a mention.

CHAPTER SIX

The Reunion

WHEN THE FIVE-YEAR HIGH school reunion came up, at first I was reluctant to go. I was just barely in touch with Miranda and Denise, and I didn't really have any other friends from school, not close ones anyway. I mean, there was that period of time when Denise went away to live in Philadelphia. My only real friend left at that time was Miranda, and all she wanted to do was to hang out with her football-playing boyfriend, Dan. I liked Dan, but he never had much to say. Neither did I, so we used to wind up just listening to Miranda going on and on. I tried hanging around with Nancy, a nice girl who used to talk to Miranda a lot. I liked her, but she started nagging me to tell Miranda to stop drinking so much. I explained to her once that I did tell both Miranda and Denise that they shouldn't drink so much, but neither of them listened to me at all, so it seemed like a waste of time to keep bothering them.

When Nancy kept nagging me anyway, I started finding other ways to spend my time. Usually that was staying home, making cookies with my Mom and snuggling on the bed with our gray cat, Norton. I loved reading, and my favorite book was *One Hundred and One Dalmatians*, but I also liked *The Catcher in the Rye*, *Little Women*, and the books about Narnia. When my sister brought *Atlas Shrugged* home, I gave it a look, but didn't really like it much. I often had the radio on, and I was crazy about Frankie Lymon and Buddy Holly. It broke my heart when he died, like everyone else, I guess. And Sam Cooke, another one that died too young, and of course, Elvis. It was a good time for music.

They played a lot of that music at the reunion, of course. There were some more modern songs, like from the Beatles, but people wanted to hear their favorite music from high school. That was the best thing about going. Mainly, it was Denise who talked me into going. She didn't want to go by herself, feeling bad about still being single. I eventually agreed, even though I dreaded seeing John Smith. Denise said that she would "protect me," but I knew better. Unless by "protect" she really meant chasing John Smith around all night. As it turned out, he didn't really seem to notice me, or her for that matter, which suited me just fine.

My first memory of that night was helping Denise get ready. I was wearing my one nice dress, a blue cotton floral with a full, pleated skirt and cute little matching belt. Denise bought a black sleeveless sheath dress, like Audrey Hepburn in *Breakfast at Tiffany's,* but shorter. She kept asking if it was too much, and I said it was perfect since she really did look like a taller Audrey Hepburn in it. Then she said her heels were too high and wanted to wear mine. I wasn't going for that because I couldn't walk in those shoes of hers and she would stretch out my nice little patent leather kitten heels with her big old feet. Finally, she decided to wear some patent leather flats with cute phony buckles she had lying around. She was afraid she would trip in the heels and she was probably right about that. Finally, we got to the makeup and she couldn't decide about her lipstick. I said that of course she had to wear red lipstick with a black dress, and it looked great on her. I was wearing pink because I always did, that's all. "So, you want to look amazing but you're nervous, right?" I asked her, and she said, "I just don't want to make a fool of myself, you know? You remember how I always liked John Smith, and he'll be there. He was supposed to go back to Vietnam but there was some problem, I think."

"When was he even in Vietnam?" I asked, "I didn't know that we were sending people there until just recently,"

"He was with some special operation where they were helping the South Vietnamese. I don't know much about it. Anyway, he came home but he was telling everyone that he was going back again. With what's going on there now, I guess maybe he wants to be there, the way he talks about it."

"Do you suppose he got into some kind of trouble?" I asked, thinking, that wouldn't be anything new.

"I have no idea. But I saw him not long ago at the store. He was in his car, I didn't talk to him. But he grew a beard. It looks pretty cool on him."

"Pretty cool for a total jerk, you mean. You need to leave him alone, Denise. You know what he did to me," I said, giving her a look.

"I know, but he's pretty good-looking all the same, and I can't help noticing, can I? Okay, I will leave him alone," she smiled at me, "even though you won't let me wear your shoes."

"Those flats you're wearing are so cute," I said, "but I can't trade with you. My feet would be slipping out of those."

"I get it. So, could you comb my hair in the back and just make sure it looks all right?"

When we got there, it was a shock for Denise to see that John Smith had a woman with him, and they were both wearing wedding rings. I was gaping at them too, because unless it was my imagination, his wife looked a lot like a younger version of me. She was blonde and voluptuous, almost chunky, with a yard of thick hair going down her back, looking great with her pink sheath dress and matching pink pumps. She had big, round blue eyes in a round face, that made her look a bit like a pretty, blonde owl. It made me kind of queasy to realize that she actually looked like a nice girl who I would have liked to talk with if she wasn't with John Smith. What was she doing with him? I was afraid for her, unlike Denise, who was bristling with jealousy.

We found Miranda and her husband, Dan. He looked uncomfortable in a black suit that was a little too small for his big, tall body. Miranda looked adorable even though Denise and I were surprised to see that she was actually wearing her wedding dress, an ivory satin sheath dress with a wide belt. She looked at us somewhat defiantly and said, "Okay, I see you're looking at my dress. Yeah, it is my wedding dress, but that's what I got it for. I didn't want a frilly dress that I could only wear once."

"Makes sense to me," said Denise.

"I mean," I said, going slowly so I could think about what I was saying, "I remember thinking that it could have been nice if you could have got married before your first baby was born. But it worked out good this way. I loved your wedding, and you looked great."

Miranda was tapping her fingers and looked away. "I thought I told you at the time," she said, slowly and deliberately, "we got the license before Rodney was born. But I was as big as a house by then. I didn't want to look like that at my wedding."

Denise sat very still, saying nothing, and I smiled and said, "Sure, I remember now. That was a great idea. The dress is perfect. I love the ivory color with your chestnut colored hair."

Dan shot me a look and grinned a bit sheepishly. I smiled back and changed the subject. "So, you guys had another baby not that long ago? Named after you, right, Dan?"

He smiled bigger and said, "Yes he is, and it was a good call, wasn't it, Miranda?" looking at his pretty, petite wife like she was the beautiful china doll that she in fact did appear to be. She rolled her big, hazel eyes and said, "Certainly was. Another mouth-breather with chipmunk cheeks, just like you," and she planted a big kiss on her husband's face, while he beamed, with a mixture of joy and embarrassment.

He leaned back and reached for his wallet. "Look, I've got a picture," he said, and passed it to me and Denise.

It was a black and white photo of an adorable, smiling baby who certainly did have large jowly cheeks. We both exclaimed about how cute he was. "My God, Miranda," said Denise, "I could just about eat those cheeks of his. He looks delicious."

Just then, a shadow fell over the table, and I looked up to see John Smith, with his wife behind him. She leaned around him and beamed at us, while he looked only at Miranda, though he nodded at Dan. "How are you folks doing?" he asked in that low voice of his. I barely heard him, focusing on his wife, smiling at her anxiously.

"We're all right," said Dan, "how are you doing, John? Why don't you introduce us to your lady?"

"Oh," John chuckled, "Julie can introduce herself. Go ahead, babe."

She smiled even wider than before and said, "Hi, I'm Julie, so great to meet you. I'll tell you, I'm having so much fun here tonight. Everybody's been so nice…."

She was going to go on, but John touched her arm and said, "That's great. We're going to get drinks. You guys want something?"

Again, he looked at Dan and Miranda, not at me, thank God. I felt like a mouse who was waiting for the hawk's shadow to pass. "No thanks," Dan smiled, "we'll get to it."

Denise started up like she was going to speak but I grabbed her arm and gave her a slight shake of the head, and she leaned back again. Then she suddenly sat up, smiled at him and said, "Good to see you again, John."

He just looked away and pulled his wife toward the bar. "Hmmph," said Denise, "wouldn't have killed him to say, 'Good to see you too, Denise.' How about that little wife of his. Everybody's so nice, huh? Well, I'm not feeling that nice, right now."

She settled back into her chair. Then she looked at me and said, "Are you all right?"

"Yeah, I'm okay."

"All right then," said Denise, "I'm going to go get us drinks. Miranda, Dan?"

They shook their heads. "I'm only having a few beers tonight," said Dan with a smile, "I'll get our drinks later."

"Gin and tonics for us, right?" she asked me, and I said, "Make it a white wine for me."

"Well, fine for you. I need a real drink," she said, and hopped out of her chair, grabbing my pocketbook by mistake.

"Denise, that's mine," I said, holding hers out to her.

They were both patent leather, but mine had straps while hers was a clutch. "Sorry," she said, and grabbed her clutch, off to the races.

I could see her at the bar, still trying to talk to John and catch his eye, and him still ignoring her. It was almost like he was used to dealing with women like that. She finally came back and handed me my white wine. Her gin and tonic looked huge. "I got a double," she said, seeing me eyeing it, "so what?"

"That does it," said Miranda, "I need one of those too. Aren't you ready for one of your beers yet?" she asked Dan.

He smiled, looking embarrassed. "I wanted to wait, 'cause you know, once I have one, I'm going to want another, and then we'll have to leave, 'cause I can't drive after more than two."

She stared at him for a second, and said, "Well, you're just going to have to control yourself, dear. Anyway, I need a drink. I'll get you a beer, too. Be right back," and off she went, her ponytail swinging behind her.

Denise watched her go and commented, "I've always been so jealous of her hair."

"I know," I agreed, "me too, and it's funny, because brown isn't such a big deal, as hair color goes. I mean, you and I both have amazing hair, let's face it. But hers really takes the cake, and always did."

"You think that's why John always liked her so much? He's still staring at her, look at him. Even with his pretty little wife sitting right there. And I have to say, his wife looks a lot like you. Her face is different, but otherwise it could be you five years ago."

"It's creepy," I agreed.

"Am I supposed to be hearing this?" asked Dan, with a grin.

"You're supposed to keep an eye on your wife," said Denise.

"Oh, she can't stand John Smith, that doesn't bother me. Still, I wish he'd gone back to Vietnam.

It's gonna be weird for her, dealing with him being here, and I was hoping to have a nice time tonight."

I looked over toward the bar, and noticed that John Smith was talking to Miranda, and she was looking away from him, her shoulders tense. I looked back at Dan, seeing that he'd noticed this. His jaw was set, and his eyes looked troubled. Then he exclaimed, "Excuse me, ladies," smiled at us, and walked to the bar in about five paces of his big, long legs. He wedged himself between John and Miranda and started talking loudly to John.

"Wow," said Denise, "I wonder what he's saying."

"I guess they know each other pretty well from playing football," I said. "Who knows? Anyway, here comes Miranda."

Miranda had wriggled away from the bar and scooted back to our table, drink in hand. "Wow," she said, "I already had enough of that John Smith."

"What's he talking to Dan about?" asked Denise.

"Who knows?" said Miranda, "football stuff, I guess. Long as I don't have to talk to John."

"What's Dan drinking?" I wondered out loud, "that doesn't look like a beer."

"Oh, well," said Miranda, "let him have some fun. I can drive us home if I have to."

Denise sat up. "Well, I'm going over there and see what they're talking about."

I put my hand on hers and said, "Hold on, Denise. Remember what I said about that guy. Talking to him isn't going to do you any good."

"I'll be fine," she said, "I just want to see if I can get him to talk to me. I'm fed up with being ignored."

She got up, grabbed her drink and said, "Wish me luck."

I said, "I wish you would sit down."

She laughed and walked to the bar, trying to place herself between Dan and John, but they seemed to be in a heated discussion and didn't even look at her. Then she pushed her way to the bar, put her bag and drink on it, smiled up at John and said something that was loud enough that we could hear her voice, but we couldn't tell what she said. John was still ignoring her, and Dan was looking embarrassed.

Finally, she went over behind John to his wife and was talking to her in a loud, sarcastic tone. The young woman just looked at her with those big, round eyes. This seemed to get John's attention, and we saw his eyes flash as he said something to Denise, then she retorted, grabbed her drink and bag and walked back to our table again. "Wow," said Miranda, "some show this is. I wonder what he said to her. What a jerk."

Denise got to our table and flung herself into her chair, taking a long swig from her drink. Miranda asked her, "Why do you waste your time talking to that man? There're other men here, and you look stunning in that dress, I meant to say that before. You need to get over him."

I just looked at Denise, and she looked back at me, suddenly almost in tears. "Well, you did try to warn me," she said, and then sat up again, defiantly. She finished off her drink and grabbed her bag, and this time her sweater, too.

"You're right, Miranda, I need a break. I'm going somewhere else for a while. I might be back."

She took her things and stalked off to the door and left. I looked at Miranda, and asked, "Where do you think she'll go?"

She shrugged and laughed, "You know, there's at least one other reunion going on in this hotel, in the ballroom across the hall. Maybe she'll have more fun over there."

"Wow," I said.

She got up. "I'm going to the bathroom. You wanna come?"

I said, "No, I might go catch up with Nancy."

"Oh, her," Miranda laughed, "give her my regards. Tell her to have a drink on me."

I sighed. I hoped Miranda and Denise weren't going to get drunk and act stupid, but it really looked like they were headed that way. I went to where Nancy was sitting with her husband, Al. "Hi, Donna," said Nancy, "look how cute. Are we wearing the same dress? Almost," she smiled.

Indeed, she was wearing another blue floral belted dress, a lot like mine. Al said, "Great to see you, Donna."

He didn't look as happy as she did. They both had Cokes. "You guys are smart, staying off the alcohol. That's going to be my next drink," I said.

Nancy smiled and said, "You can't beat it. I saw you over there with Miranda and Denise. Where did Denise go?"

"I have no idea," I said, "and my car's at her house."

"Oh, we can give you a ride home," said Al, "Nancy doesn't like to drive at night, so I'm laying off the liquor. Are you going to your parents' house? That's right on our way."

"Thanks so much, you guys. If she doesn't come back, I might take you up on that."

"How's Pittsburgh?" asked Nancy, "life in the big city must be so exciting compared to here," and I proceeded to tell her a little about my job, and my volunteer work at the House.

"That sounds amazing," she said finally, "one of these days when our baby's older, I'd like to go up and visit you. I'd love to see that place and the wonderful work you're doing."

"How old is that baby now? Denise told me you had him, and I was so happy for you."

"He's about six months. You should see him, his personality is really developing now. Al, you've got his picture in your wallet, show Donna."

He did. As I looked, I said, "He's just adorable, and you know, I think he's about the same age as Miranda and Dan's new baby. Another boy."

Al put the picture away, looked at Nancy, then smiled at me, "That's great news. We hadn't heard that. I guess they'll be going to school together."

Nancy nodded, thoughtfully, but not really smiling. Then she said, "I'd love to talk to her about that. Where did she go?"

I looked over at our table, and Miranda was gone. Dan was still at the bar with John Smith. I shrugged and said, "I'm not sure. Maybe to the bathroom again?"

"Well when you see her, you tell her I'd love to talk to her. We want to see her baby's picture, don't we, Al?"

Al was looking at the bar wistfully. "What?" he asked, "Oh, of course we do."

I said, "If you guys are done with your Cokes, I'd love to get you another. I'm going to get one, too."

"No, thanks," said Al, but Nancy said, "I'd like another, sure. I'll come with you."

She followed me over to the table to get my pocketbook, but I was surprised to find that it wasn't there. "Oh, no," I said, "where's my pocketbook? My nice patent-leather one, I'd hate to lose it."

We looked all around the table, then the other tables nearby. One of the girls from the next table said, "I saw Denise come running in here with some older guy, and she grabbed a pocketbook, but it looked like it was hers. She thought it was, I guess."

"Do you think she made a mistake?" asked Nancy.

"Our bags do look similar, but she knows that, and she should be able to tell them apart. Anyway, I wouldn't know where to find her now. She's not even here."

Miranda showed up, and we told her what happened. "I don't think Denise would've taken your bag," she said, "She's not that drunk yet. It's probably in a garbage can somewhere. Someone wanted the money for booze."

"Aw," I said, "I like that pocketbook."

"Well," said Nancy, "let's get mine, and I'll get us a couple of Cokes. Then we'll look around some more, and if we don't find it, we'll talk to the hotel people."

I swallowed hard, and took a deep breath. I really did like my cute little pocketbook, and I was embarrassed that I had to let Nancy pay. I forced myself to smile, and said, "Sure, yeah, that sounds good."

So, we went to get the Cokes. Dan was still talking to John Smith, and I had the thought that I should try to interrupt them somehow. It looked like Dan was drinking too much, but he also looked like he was having fun, and I hated to interfere with that. Anyway, I didn't like the idea of dealing with John Smith at all, so I left them alone. We got our Cokes quickly and left, thankfully, and went around to different tables, asking if anyone had seen my pocketbook. We got a few false leads, and it looked like those little black pocketbooks were showing up all over the place, except not mine. A popular item at this reunion. Finally, we gave up and went to talk to the hotel people.

Once we stepped out of the room into the hall, we could hear the music blaring from the room across the hall. It had a piece of paper on one door with '1950 Reunion' on it. "Wow," said Nancy, "the 1950 people are listening to almost the same music as us."

"Sounds like it," I said, "That's probably where Denise went. Should we go look for her real quick, before we go to the hotel desk?"

"I'm game if you are," said Nancy with a grin, and I grinned back.

"Okay, here goes nothing," I said, opening the door as we both snuck in. We blinked a little in the darkened room, and looked around. "I don't see Denise," I said.

"Me neither," said Nancy, "let's just ask someone."

A couple of men walked past us holding beers, so I asked them, "Hey, did you happen to see our friend? From the 1960 reunion across the hall? She's tall, with a black dress?"

One of them looked at the other, smiled at us and asked, "A pretty young lady with dark hair?"

I said yes, and he said to his friend, "that was the girl who was talking to Chuck, right?"

Then he turned to me and said, "She was talking to our friend and they seem to have gone somewhere, but we have no idea where. You ladies want to join us? We can get you something stronger than those Cokes."

"No, thanks," said Nancy, "but we appreciate your help. Come on, Donna," she pulled me toward the door, but I didn't need pulling, I was right behind her.

"Well," she said to me, once we were out in the hall again, "I guess that's it with Denise. We won't be seeing her again tonight. Al and I can take you home, like we were saying."

"Wow," I said, "I hope she's okay. Oh, well. You think we should look in the bathroom?"

"I guess it can't hurt."

The bathroom was a nice one, with a sitting room with a long vanity shelf with a mirror, with several bottles of lotion and perfume, a box of tissues and a little basket for tips. We put a few quarters in that and looked under the doors of the stalls to see if Denise's black buckled flats showed up, but they didn't. We did see another pair of black pumps that looked like Miranda's, and the door swung open and out she came, wiping her mouth with toilet paper and stopping short when she saw us. "Oh, hey, you guys," she said, and tried to smile, "you know, I guess I'm not feeling too good."

"Sorry to hear that, sweetie," I said, taking her arm, "come on and sit in one of these chairs over here."

We all sat down and Miranda said, "I guess I didn't really eat dinner, I was so excited about coming here, but that was a mistake. Two gin and tonics and I'm puking my guts out."

"We're looking for Denise," said Nancy, "and it turns out she went somewhere with some guy from the 1950 reunion."

Miranda bent over laughing. Then she sat up and said, "Donna, can you hand me those tissues?"

I did, and she started wiping her face. "Oh, man," she said, "that is so funny. Well, I hope she's having a good time. Did either of you bring mascara? I gotta fix my face. All I brought was a lipstick."

"No purse," I said, but Nancy chimed in, "You can use mine," and handed her a tube from her purse.

"Thanks," said Miranda, and went over to the mirror.

Nancy smiled at her and said, "Donna mentioned that you and Dan had a baby a few months ago. You know, I just had my first, he's six months old now."

"Wow," said Miranda, "we both have boys about the same age. Dan's the one that carries the baby's picture in his wallet, I'll get him to show you if he ever stops drinking tonight."

She took her hair out of the ponytail and started combing it. Then she looked at me in the mirror and asked. "Am I right, is Dan still drinking with John?"

"Yes," I said, "and I have to say, he looked like he was enjoying himself. Poor little John Smith's wife was just sitting next to him looking bored while he was carrying on with Dan. I felt sorry for her, a little."

"So weird that he is married to someone who looks so much like you," said Miranda, "did I say that already?"

"I think maybe Denise did. I don't want to talk about that. Will you and Dan be able to get home okay?"

"Oh, sure, I mean, I'm not going to drink anymore after this. In fact, I'm gonna go get him to go home pretty soon. I've had it, I feel lousy."

Nancy stood up, looking concerned. "Well, we better go talk to the hotel people. We still didn't find Donna's purse. We can give you a ride if you need one, Miranda. We're taking Donna home but there's room for you and Dan, too. The backseat is big enough for three people."

"No, that's okay, but thanks anyway. I'll be fine to drive home. You guys go on ahead. Oh, here's your mascara."

"Don't worry, I have another one at home," said Nancy with a smile, "See you later, Miranda," and we shuffled out.

We went down the hall to the hotel entrance, where the main desk was. There was an older woman behind the desk with her hair pulled back and big pink wing-tipped glasses. She pursed her lips at us, with matching pink lipstick, and said, "Yes?"

We explained about the pocketbook, and I said my friend might have taken it by mistake, but we couldn't find her. She frowned slightly and picked up the phone. "When property goes missing, we contact the police," she said to us around the phone, and then said "hello" into it with a much nicer voice, presumably talking to the police.

I turned to Nancy, rolled my eyes, and said, "This looks like it's going to take a while. You go on back and see how Al's doing, I'm fine to wait here."

So, she did, and when the lady got off the phone, she told me to go outside to wait for the police. Good thing I brought my sweater, a cream-colored wool cardigan. I pulled it on as I went out. There was a nice little fake pond with a fountain in the middle, in front of the entrance, with benches along the sidewalk, closer to the hotel. I sat on one of those, over to the side, where I could see the entrance but wouldn't be noticed by people going in. I wanted to be quiet for a while. As I looked around, I thought I saw Al farther along on another bench, and I smelled something I hadn't smelled since that party in my first year of nursing school. *Wow*, I was thinking, *Nancy wouldn't like it. But hey, it's none of my business*, and I started to get up to move away so he wouldn't notice me.

Just then, John Smith came out of the hotel, dragging Dan by the lapel of his tight, black suit. "Come on, you S.O.B., can't hold your liquor," John roared, and I froze, thinking they must be fighting.

But then I saw that Dan was giggling hysterically. "Slow down, John, you big bastard," he yelled back, but his speech was so slurred I almost couldn't tell what he was saying.

John yelled out, "No way, you fat drunk. You wanna get sober, this is how you do it," and he plunged into the fountain and dragged Dan with him, yelling, "You gotta get your head right under the water," and grabbed Dan by the collar.

"Oh, no, you don't," yelled Dan, and pulled back, but John grabbed him by the arm this time. It looked like he was trying some wrestling move. I turned and noticed Al was approaching, with something in his hand. He saw me and waved, but kept staring at John and Dan.

Then Miranda came out of the hotel, shrieking like a boiling kettle. "What's going on here?" she screamed, and ran right over to the fountain, jumping in with them. She took her pocketbook and went to hit John Smith with it, but she fell and went right down in the water, even dunking her head in it. She came up sputtering, scrambled up and started hitting John again, yelling, "You let him go, you horrible man," and this was when the police car pulled up the drive. The policeman jumped up and ran over, and out of the corner of my eye I saw Al dropping something and stomping on it, easing himself slowly to the hotel entrance and sneaking in. The policeman went over to the fountain and helped Miranda out. John Smith, whose face had gone hard as a rock, stole a glance at the policeman and left. The policeman looked back at him but just nodded, and he asked Miranda and Dan what happened. Dan said, "Don't worry, officer, John and me were just fooling around, and I guess Miranda got upset. You okay, baby?" he asked her, and she said, "I just want to go get my sweater and leave."

"Okay, Miranda," said Dan, and turning to the policeman, asked, "is it okay if we leave? Everything's fine, really."

"Yes, I guess it's fine as long as you're both okay. I came here about a stolen pocketbook. You know anything about that?"

"That's my pocketbook, officer," I said, and approached them. Dan and Miranda looked embarrassed when they saw me, and slunk away as fast as they could manage. As I got closer, I saw that the policeman looked a little familiar. I asked him, "Do you work in Possumtown? Have I seen you there?"

He said, "Yes, that's where I usually work, but I was asked to come out here today because they were down a few people. I guess there's a virus going around."

"Now I know," I said, "you came to the A&W that time, when my parents called the police 'cause I wasn't home yet. Do you remember that? I'm pretty sure it was you. My sister showed up and took me home. She was flirting with you a little," I laughed.

"Oh, yeah, now I remember. Your parents called the police station when you didn't come straight home from school. You must've been home every day like clockwork most of the time."

I laughed again and said, "Listen, it's possible that my friend took my pocketbook by mistake, but I couldn't find her because she left. It wasn't my idea to call the police. The lady at the desk did that."

"Oh, I get it," he said, "Did you look around for it already? Okay, I'm going to go talk to that desk lady. You don't have to wait around. I'll take your information and you'll be contacted if we find it. But if your friend does turn out to have it, I'd appreciate it if you let me know. Best way is to call the Possumtown police station, ask for Ed, that's me. Now, do you have a ride home?"

"Yeah, my friends said they would take me. Thanks, I better go and find them," I said, and I headed back to the reunion.

Al and Nancy were waiting for me, and Al drove us back to Possumtown. It was funny to me that he drove kind of slowly. I wondered if he was experiencing anything like what I experienced when I drove home after that party in Pittsburgh, back in my first year of nursing school, but of course, I couldn't ask him. I did ask them if they saw Miranda and Dan before they left, and Nancy said that they had showed up just briefly for Miranda to get her sweater, then left without saying good-bye to anyone. "I wanted to see her baby's picture. It's too bad, I don't know when I'll run into her again," said Nancy.

"You could call her," I suggested.

"I suppose so," said Nancy, sounding doubtful.

"Okay," said Al, "this is your stop, Donna," as he pulled up into my parents' driveway.

"Would you guys like to come in for coffee?" I asked them.

"Oh, no thanks," said Nancy, "We have to get home. Al's mom is with the baby."

"Well, thanks so much for taking me home. It was great spending time with you, too. I'm gonna stay in touch, okay?"

"That would be great," said Al, and they both smiled at me.

It felt so good to be home after that long, crazy night. I let myself in quietly, tiptoed upstairs and got into my old bed, where I used to sleep when I was growing up. It felt like an old friend. The next morning, I called Denise over my first cup of coffee. It was only nine o'clock, but I figured she'd probably be awake, and anyway I wanted to know about my pocketbook. "Hey, Denise, did you wind up with two pocketbooks last night by any chance?"

"No," she said, "but the one that I have is yours. I guess I must have lost mine, and then I thought I'd left it behind, so I went and grabbed yours by mistake. Sorry about that."

"So, you have mine there? That's great," I said, "I'll come over and get it. You know, my car is still at your house, so my Dad has to drive me, and he won't go anywhere until he has his breakfast and coffee, so it will be at least an hour."

"Well, you can take as long as you want," she said, "I'm not going anywhere. I have a splitting headache."

"By the way, you might want to contact the Possumtown police about your lost pocketbook. The policeman who came to the hotel about it was from here, not from town."

"I don't know when I'll get around to dealing with that. Right now, I'm going back to bed with some Alka-Seltzer."

"I hope that works out for you," I chuckled, and we hung up.

I called the Possumtown police myself, and I asked for Ed. He wasn't there, so I left him a message. Then I got up, got myself another cup of coffee and looked out the kitchen window at the sun on the trees. What a night. I remember telling myself I was gonna skip the next reunion. And so far, I've never been back to another one.

CHAPTER SEVEN

Penny and Her Mom

AFTER THE REUNION, I wasn't so eager to go back to Possumtown that much. I went to see my parents, of course, and my sister Karen and her daughter, my wonderful niece Mandy, at least once, or maybe a couple of times, a month or so. I didn't have time to go more than that, because of my volunteer work at the Catholic Worker House. It was actually easier to find time for visiting after I started my job as Lay Worker, and went from just spending a day at the House, once a week or so, to working there all week long. That was when Jenny decided to quit working there so she could spend more time with her grandchildren, late in 1972. It made a big change for me, spending all my working days at the House, and it took me a while to get used to that, although I loved working there.

It wasn't long after that, in fact it was a few weeks before Christmas, when I ran into Penny, the girl who I'd last seen when we dropped her off at her mother's house in that ambulance. I remembered that the house was in Canonsberg, so I never expected to run into her in town, especially in my own neighborhood. I walked into a local dime store to buy candy for my niece, and there was Penny. She was wearing a heavy parka with a scarf and hat, but I saw her pretty blue eyes and right away I knew who she was.

"Penny," I cried, smiling and sort of peering at her to gauge her reaction to seeing me again. "Hi," I continued, "remember me, Donna, from the ER at University Hospital? It's been maybe ten years so you might not recognize me."

She looked a little stunned at first, and a number of emotions passed across her face. Then she put a hand over her mouth and gasped, "Oh, my God," and staggered over to me, holding her arms out for a hug.

"You saved my life," she said to the side of my head as she threw her arms around me.

Then she backed up and looked at me. "Wow, you don't look a bit different, Donna. I bet I do, right? I'm surprised you even recognized me."

"Well," I said, "you look a lot healthier and happier."

"Yeah," she said, "I put on weight."

"Good thing," I said laughing, "You were so tiny. What are you doing out here in Oakland? Don't you live in Canonsberg?"

"I'm studying to be a nurse, like you. I'm getting a late start, after going to a community college and taking forever to decide what I wanted to do. But there was free career counseling at the school, and after a few sessions I thought about you and what you did for me, and I knew I wanted to be a nurse."

"Wow," I said, almost beginning to cry, "that is so great. I know you will be a really good one. Let's get together sometime and talk about nursing school. I'd love to hear how it's going for you."

"I would love that. Are you doing anything tonight? I want you to come over and have dinner with me and Mom, and I know when I tell her I ran into you, she will want to have you over right away. She still talks about you, and how grateful she was that you guys brought me home."

"I was grateful that we could do it. Sure, I guess I can come over. You have to give me your address, 'cause I totally forgot where you guys live, I just remember Canonsberg. What time should I show up?"

"Six o'clock, and don't eat between now and then, she's going to make a whole bunch of food. I can't wait to tell her you're coming."

So, later that evening, I found myself sitting at a grey linoleum table in Penny's mother's kitchen. We had some coffee and talked about nursing school for at least an hour while her mom finished making dinner. Then we shared a wonderful meal of fried chicken with corn, green beans and mashed potatoes with gravy on the side. I could feel my stomach expanding and silently thanked myself for not wearing jeans that day, or I would have had to unsnap them. "I can't remember when I last ate that much," I smiled at

Penny's mother, "the vegetables taste so fresh. Did you can them yourself?"

(By this, I meant, preserving the vegetables in Mason jars. We referred to this as canning, even though we didn't use actual cans, because it comes to much the same thing. Except it's a lot better than actual canned vegetables, of course.)

"Why, yes I did," she said with a smile, "and we were lucky to get them. See, we don't have enough room in the yard for a real garden, just some tomatoes and peppers and such. But I have a cousin who lives on a farm out west of here, and they have such a big garden, they usually get me out there during the summer, and they say, pick as much as you want, so we do and then we bring it back and freeze it or can it as soon as we get the chance."

"Wow, I'm so lucky to be eating them. They sure taste great."

She replied, "If you're finished, I'll take your plate. Want some coffee?"

Once we were all settled with our coffee cups, Penny said, "We are just always so grateful to you for getting me out of that awful situation."

I smiled and said, "Well, helping you was the least I could do. But it was amazing how that nurse got us on that ambulance. Sorry to say, I've forgotten her name, but she really made it happen, God bless her."

Penny's mom chimed in, "I think about it every day, how grateful I was to get my girl back. My ex-husband was … I mean, I hate to talk about what he was doing to my girl," and tears came to her eyes.

Penny looked at her mom lovingly and said, "I'm just so glad you finally believed me. It's okay now, Mom."

The older woman looked up and said, "I threw him out, after she left. He finally admitted what he was doing, and I think he really thought I would let him stay, but I got him out of here, all right. My cousin, the one with the garden, helped me with that. And then, I was frantic to get my girl back, but the police weren't doing much to help, as far as I could tell. So, when she called me from the hospital, I was crying, I was so glad to hear from her."

I smiled at her, and looked at Penny, asking her, "Did you have any trouble from that man who was chasing you, that day?"

"My friend, the one that brought me to the hospital, she called me once and told me the man got thrown in jail for something else, and he's gonna be there for a long time. I think she wanted me to come back, but I wouldn't, of course. I even told her she could come here if she wanted, but she said no. She said she'd keep in touch, but I never heard from her again. I pray for her sometimes."

"I can light a candle for her at the House. What's her name?"

"Joanna," she said.

"It happened to me, too, when I was young," said her mother, eyeing me cautiously, "my uncle messed around with me, and I tried to tell my parents about it, but they wouldn't listen. I think that's why I got married so young, to get out of the house. In fact, I married my first boyfriend from high school, we were both just eighteen. That was her father," she looked at Penny.

"But," she continued, "we were both so young, the marriage didn't last. Then years later I met my second husband, what a mistake I made, marrying him. That's the man that was messing with my girl, I still can't believe that I couldn't see what was happening. And you know, when I look back on it, I think he may have been interested in me just to get at Penny," she finished, and began crying again.

Penny held her hand and said, "Mom."

I patted the woman on the shoulder, and said, "These things happen to so many of us. I was raped in high school by a boy I knew, and I've always blamed myself, because I got into his car. But I didn't know what would happen, or want it to, at all. And when I listen to you, I can see that we're not to blame that these things happened to us. It's funny that I can see that better when I'm hearing someone else's story."

Penny's mom was still sobbing a little. "It's like, we don't talk about it 'cause we're worried about what people will think. But maybe it happened to them too, but you can't know 'cause nobody's talking," she finished as she wiped her face with a tissue.

"The important thing is, we're all okay now. Thank God for that. Sorry to say, I probably better head back home, soon. It'll be late by the time I get back to my apartment."

"Oh, yeah," said Penny, "you want to get home before it gets too late. We like to watch *The Bold Ones*, at nine thirty. Do you ever watch that show?"

"That's the one with *The Doctors*, right?" I laughed, "you know, it's good, but I liked *The Lawyers* episodes better. I had a crush on that James Farentino."

"Really?" said Penny, "I never thought he was that cute," but her mother was laughing and said, "I'm with Donna on that one."

"Well," said Penny, "Mom, you like that Jack Lord, too. Sometimes," she said to Donna, "I can't get her to change the channel when she's watching *Hawaii Five-O,* and then *The Bold Ones* comes on."

I laughed, "I kind of get your Mom, though. That's a tough choice."

We talked some more about nursing school, and it turned out that Penny was taking a class on neurological conditions, including alcoholism. She said she needed to do some fieldwork to learn more about it, so I suggested she might want to come and take a look at the Worker House. She loved that idea, and we agreed to call each other and work out a good time for that. Then I thanked them both again as I walked out. It was chilly, and I pulled a knit hat out of my bag and put it on my head, even though it was just a short walk to my car. Getting into Pittsburgh, I had the thought that it might be good to stop by at the House and see if Father Douglas was still around.

CHAPTER EIGHT

The Poet

IT WAS KIND OF late, maybe almost nine o'clock, when I got back to Pittsburgh, but I wanted to check at the House to see if Father Douglas was still up. I wanted to make sure he was okay with my idea of inviting Penny to come to the House for her field-work assignment. I could have waited, but if by some chance he wasn't happy with the idea, I wanted to be able to let Penny know soon, so she wouldn't be too disappointed.

As I got closer to the House, I saw a man walking toward it, going up to the door, looking at it, then going back to the sidewalk. I parked my car, walked toward him and asked him what he was looking for.

"Is this the place for homeless people?" he asked, "I'm looking for a place to stay. My parents kicked me out."

"Well, it's kind of late for an intake, the men are going to bed soon, but let's see if there's someone inside who can help you," I said, as I walked up and opened the door.

I knew it would be open, since they don't lock the doors until nine o'clock. I walked in and let him in behind me, then I motioned for him to go down the hall to where there were lights on, in the kitchen in the back of the building. "Hey, Yves," I called into the kitchen, "can you get this young man a cup of coffee, or something, while I go look for Father Douglas?"

"Sure, wow, you were lucky," Yves said to the man, "another five minutes or so and the door would be locked. Take a seat in the dining room, right over there, and I'll bring you something."

He motioned to a doorway and turned on a light switch to a room with long tables and chairs. "Right over there," he smiled at the man, and I smiled at him too, asking, "What's your name?"

"Rick," he said, blinking from behind black-rimmed glasses, his eyes almost bulging behind them, his face pink from the cold.

He had no hat, and his brown hair was thin in front. "Okay, Rick, Yves will get you something and I'm going to get Father Douglas. He needs to speak with you for a few minutes and then we'll find you a place to sleep."

"Oh, that sounds great," he said, "I was so worried. It's too cold to sleep outdoors tonight, you know? I didn't know where to go until some guy downtown told me about this place. I couldn't cover bus fare for the whole trip, I guess I walked at least a mile."

"Well, get some hot coffee in you," said Yves, putting a cup on the table for him, "you take milk or sugar?"

"No, thanks," Rick said, "this is great." He held the cup in his hands, to warm them.

"I'll be back soon," I said, smiling again, and went back down the hall toward the front, where another door on the right took me to the waiting room in front of Father Douglas' office, where I'd first met Jenny, years before. I peeked in to see what Father Douglas was doing. He was on the phone, but when he saw me, he said, "Wait a minute," lowered the phone and asked me, "Someone here?"

"A guy just showed up. I saw him outside. He's in the dining room, Yves is giving him coffee and something to eat."

"Okay, get him to fill out the form and I'll be there in just a minute."

I got the intake form from a folder on Father Douglas' desk and went back to the kitchen. I gave the form to Rick, with a pen, and said, "Just fill out whatever you can, okay? After you've warmed up a bit and had your food. Your hands must have been cold."

He had gloves, but they looked a little too thin for this weather, and he was still visibly shaking from spending hours out in the cold. "This coffee really helps, thanks," he looked up at me guardedly, and asked, "You work here?"

"Yes," I said, "I used to be a volunteer, but recently I started working here full time. We've had so many men coming here, quite a few are veterans, I think you'll find."

"Veterans, wow. They've been through a lot. I run into lots of them outside, too. Course, I have my own stories to tell. I write poems, you know."

"Wow," I said, "I'd like to see them sometime. Are you from around here?"

"My parents are living in Possumtown. It's a little place, not far from Harrisburg."

"That's where I'm from," I beamed, "I wonder if we know anybody in common."

"Oh, naw, I doubt it. I'm too old for that high school, the only people I've met are a few of the neighbors and the minister of that Presbyterian church my parents go to. But that's in town. It's funny, I've hardly ever even been to Possumtown, really, even though my Dad's farm is close to it. But none of us like living there, except my Dad, and maybe my little sister, but she's too young to get a vote. And wouldn't you know, they're leaving pretty soon."

"They're moving away? Where?"

"Well, my Dad got a chance to work in England, see? He works selling insurance to military people, and they have those American bases in England and Germany, so they're sending him to sell insurance over there."

"Wow, are you going with them?"

"No," he said, laughing a little, "I think part of the whole idea was to get away from me, if you want to know the truth."

He was blinking at me again, but his look was almost confrontational.

"Why would they do that?" I asked gently.

"I don't know," he said, sounding exasperated, "I guess they think I make problems for them. They sent me to the State Hospital in Dayton, where we used to live, and then again to Harrisburg State, just a few months ago. But I'm on medication now, and I don't make trouble, don't worry."

I just looked at him for a minute, feeling sad, and wondering if we should be taking him. He wasn't our first to have a mental-illness history, but he sounded like he could have a serious problem, and it wasn't something I felt totally qualified to deal with. Still, he needed a place to sleep, so we could give him that, at least for a while. Father Douglas showed up, and I took the opportunity to say good night and leave.

CHAPTER NINE

A Misunderstanding

WHEN I SHOWED UP the next day to help with breakfast, there was Rick, coming back to the kitchen for seconds on everything, especially the bacon. Yves chuckled and told him to take it easy, at which Rick just blinked, making off with his plate of food like it was a bag of diamonds. "That boy could eat," Yves commented to me with a smile, adding, "it's nice to see someone enjoying the food around here."

"Everybody likes your food, Yves," I said, laughing, "even me, and I'm pretty fussy. My mom's a really good cook."

"Too bad she didn't teach you more about that," commented Yves, looking at me sideways while he was taking bacon off the grill.

"Well, yeah, I guess I always had my head in a book. My sister got the cooking lessons, not me."

"Never mind, young lady. You just help me with the plates and such, I can handle the rest. Only, I need you to help with chopping vegetables again today. Some fancy downtown restaurant is giving Father Douglas their leftovers for us and it sounds like good stuff, so we have to use it fast, you know?"

"Sure, that'll be fine. I just have to ask Father Douglas if he has any paperwork that he needs done this morning, after that I can chop all the vegetables you want."

Yves was a good guy to work with, and I guess he had to be patient, too, dealing with all these men as well as his wife and five kids. I went to Father Douglas' office to check about the paperwork and there was Rick again, standing by Father Douglas' desk with his hands in his pockets, talking intensely about something I couldn't hear. "Wow," I said, "how did you get here so fast? I thought you were still eating."

He hesitated a second or two, then grinned and said, "Oh, man, that was some breakfast. I haven't eaten like that since I left home, a few weeks back."

Father Douglas smiled, looked at me and said, "Rick was telling me he was living near Possumtown. That's where you're from, right?"

"Yes," I said, "we were talking about that, too. But Rick, I didn't get around to asking you: is there a specific reason you left home?"

He looked down, heaved a sigh, pulled his hands out of his pockets, examined his fingernails, then looked up and said, "They wanted to send me back to Harrisburg State."

"Why?" I asked, but Father Douglas was signaling for me to be quiet.

"They thought I wasn't taking my meds. They said, 'You need to have your meds adjusted,' but I know they thought I wasn't taking them. I never do that. I always take my meds. They told me that, to make sure to take them, first time I was in the hospital, and I always do," he finished, looking at us very seriously over his glasses.

"Do you have them with you?" asked Father Douglas, and Rick said yes and pulled a container of prescription pills out of his left front jeans pocket. Father Douglas looked at them for a minute, and said, "Well, I'm going to write down the doctor's name and number, just for future reference, but I think this looks okay. Of course, if you're going to stay here, we'll need to send you for a psychiatric evaluation at some point soon. Donna can set that up, she's a nurse, you know."

"Oh wow, well, that sounds fine," he said, looking at us both with a sort of half-smile on his face.

"Anything else you need for me to work on, Father, before I go help Yves in the kitchen?" I asked.

"There is one thing. Could you go in the chapel and see if I left my notebook behind the altar? I can't find it and I was wondering if I left it there."

"Sure, Father, I'll go look right now," I said, heading back toward the kitchen but going through a door on the left this time. There was the chapel, about half the size of the church I went to in Possumtown, but big enough for the men here, maybe about fifty feet long by twenty feet wide, with a modest but well-kept altar and a rather beautiful, if stark, crucifix that had been carved in wood by someone who gifted the face a moving expression of pain mixed with ecstasy. I loved that crucifix, and always bowed and said a brief prayer in front of it. I wasn't raised Catholic, but I saw Father Douglas doing this and it felt right to do it also. Doing that now, thinking I was completely alone, I prayed the Our Father and then started my list of people I prayed for: my mother and father, sister Karen and niece Mandy, and my friends Miranda and Denise, with their alcohol problems and neglected kids. This time I prayed for Penny and her lost friend, Joanna, and then I was considering what Father Douglas had suggested to me once, about praying for John Smith, of all people, but thinking about this clouded my mind.

At just that point, I felt someone tapping my shoulder, and whirled around, feeling a shock of adrenaline go through me. It was Rick, and he was much too close for comfort. Without thinking, I found myself screaming, "Get away from me. Don't touch me. What do you think you're doing?" as I backed toward the altar. It seemed like someone else was screaming with a strangled and desperate wail. My mind was barely taking in what was happening.

The young man backed away from me with his face contorted in revulsion. "I barely touched you, lady. What is wrong with you? I just wanted to ask a simple question, is all. Just, where's the bathroom on this floor, that's all I wanted to know. What's wrong with you? I didn't do anything to you."

He almost started sobbing and his expression went in a flash from revulsion to fear. "If they kick me out of here because of this ...." He didn't finish the sentence, just looked around in anguish, kicked the pew next to him and then gripped the back of it and breathed heavily, counting "one, two ...."

I came back to where I was and realized he was trying to calm himself. *I got him all upset*, I thought, *why did I do that? Why did I react that way?* I began breathing too, in a slow rhythm, and after about a minute, I felt like maybe I could speak to him again. "I'm sorry," I said quietly, "that was a mistake I made. I can see you meant no harm."

He still wasn't looking at me or turning around, but he stopped counting and seemed to be listening, so I went on. "I see that I overreacted. I hope you will forgive me for that. Something happened to me when I was younger, and that makes some situations difficult for me now."

He stood, still not looking at me, and began to speak gruffly. "Okay, I get it, you were raped or something. That's it, right?"

I sighed and simply said, "Yes, that's right."

"Well," he said, "I'm sorry that happened to you. But you're not the only one in the world, you know? Believe it or not, even men get raped, too."

I registered this, and after turning it over in my mind, I said, "This happened to you?"

"Yes, it did," he said with harsh emphasis. I wanted to ask him when and where, but he had his face turned, and I could see that his expression was contorted in an effort to control himself. A sort of hiccuping sob came from his diaphragm, then another. I waited to see if he would get calm. After another minute or two, the sobs subsided, and with a deep sigh, he looked at me.

Such an expression of pain was on his young face that I wanted to hug him, but instead I gently asked,

"Could we talk about this? Let's sit down and have some coffee."

He looked away, thinking, and heaved another sigh. "Okay, why not," he said, "course, I have to use the bathroom first."

We both shuffled out of the chapel, and I showed him where the restroom was, and said I would wait for him in the dining room. I went to the kitchen to see if Yves had coffee on. Yves glanced at me, saying, "I heard something. Is everything okay?"

I sighed. "That new guy, Rick, came to ask me something in the chapel and I didn't see him until he tapped me on the shoulder. I guess he scared me, I don't even know why I got so upset. And you know, I forgot all about Father Douglas' notebook."

"Well, if you need help, just come back in here and give me a look. I like that young man, but he does appear to be a bit of hard work."

I think I said already that Yves was from Jamaica, and sometimes he used language that wasn't familiar to me. He told me once that it was because he had a British education.

"Thanks, Yves," I said, "I'm gonna try to talk with him. He does seem like a good kid. I'm going for Father Douglas' notebook first. Could you take the coffee to Rick and make sure he waits for me? I don't want him to wander off somewhere."

"Sure," said Yves, "I'd like to talk with him. Can't help wondering why his family kicked him out," he shook his head slightly.

"Me too," I said, and went back to the chapel. There indeed was the notebook, and I picked it up and sort of walked-ran it back to Father Douglas.

He was looking over some papers and didn't look up when I came in. I said, "Here, Father Douglas," and put it on his desk, and he looked up, blinking.

Then he smiled and said, "Oh, thank you. I was wondering where I put it. Is everything okay? I thought I heard yelling."

"I had a misunderstanding with the new guy. He surprised me and I got upset. You know, I'm not even sure why I got that upset." Suddenly tears were in my eyes, and I blinked them back.

"Do you need me to come and talk to him?" asked Father Douglas, looking at me intently.

"No, I think I can talk to him myself. He didn't mean any harm, I just over-reacted. You know what, I was trying what you suggested, praying for that guy, John Smith. Maybe because I was thinking about that...."

"That could have put you in a state of mind to be easily upset by something, I can see that. Well, too bad you guys had a problem. Even so, I am proud of you for following my suggestion. That took courage."

"But you know, I couldn't do it. I couldn't pray for him, Father. I was thinking about it, but I couldn't."

He looked at me reflectively, and said, "Well, even thinking about it is a start. And if it's hard to do, then I am even more proud of you for trying. God is helping you with this, Donna."

Suddenly, I sat in a chair, taking a tissue from a box on his desk. I thought I was going to cry again, but somehow instead, my mind just went blank, and I felt numb. I sighed again, then looked at Father Douglas and said, "I hope you're right. Anyway, I'm going to talk with Rick. You know what he told me?

He was raped, too. I'm only saying this to you, Father," I added, looking around to make sure the door was shut.

When I looked back, Father Douglas was looking at me, calmly but intently, as he did when he wanted us to pay attention. He said, "Well, you two have a lot to talk about, then. God be with you. I'm here to help if you need it."

"Thank you, Father," I said, getting up, and taking another tissue.

"Take the box," he said, pushing it toward me.

CHAPTER TEN

Blondes Can Be Writers

I WALKED INTO THE dining room. Rick was sitting with his back toward me, facing the windows along the far wall of the room, his head propped on his hands. I couldn't see his face and I hoped he wasn't crying, but then again, I did have that box of tissues. I walked up to the table and put the tissue box down quietly on the seat, hoping he wouldn't see it, because I didn't want him to think I expected either of us to need them. I went to get another cup of coffee for him, remembering that he liked it black. I was hesitating, a little. Actually, I wasn't used to this. I had brief conversations with the men every day, but I was usually too busy to talk for long, and I preferred it that way, thinking it was better not to get too close to them.

Apart from Grace, an older woman who did some of the cleaning and laundry, I was the only woman in the House, since Jenny retired, and it seemed appropriate to keep a certain distance.

So, I felt awkward. I said, "Hi Rick, here's your coffee," put down his cup, and then suddenly I decided I wanted some coffee, too. I said, "I guess I'll get some after all. You sure you don't want cream or sugar?"

"No, I take it like this," he said.

"Okay, I'll be right back," I said.

Once I had another cup of coffee ready, I was still wondering how to start the conversation. I sat down and looked at him. He was looking at his coffee. I said, "Didn't you say you're from Ohio?"

"Yeah, Dayton," he responded.

"And your family's in Possumtown now. When did you guys move?"

"A couple of years ago, but we moved to a place near Philadelphia. We've only been on the farm since last summer. I think I told somebody about that already, maybe it was Father Douglas. My parents wanted to get me into some program out by Philadelphia, but it didn't turn out to be that great, in the end. They pulled me out, and I left home, came back, left again, came back again. Then we moved to that farm."

He got a disgusted look on his face. "You don't like it there?" I asked.

"Course not. It's miles away from anything. Nobody likes it, except my Dad. And maybe my little sister, but I'm not even sure, 'cause we hardly ever talk anymore."

"How come? You guys don't get along?"

"I don't know. Seems like she used to talk to me. But I guess I used to yell at her sometimes, and my little brother too. I just needed for them to leave me alone."

"Was that when you started with the …."

"The schizophrenia, right, or that's what they called it, anyway. And my parents let this doctor put me in the mental hospital, Dayton State. That's where it happened. I was only seventeen, but they put me in with the adults, where I shouldn't have been. And that's about all I want to say about that, hope you don't mind if I leave out the details."

"I'm sorry. Your parents must have felt terrible."

"Maybe they did. Still their fault, anyway. They shouldn't have let them put me in there like that."

"I guess they thought those people knew what they were doing."

"Well, they thought wrong, if that's what they thought. Anyway, what happened to you? You got raped, too, right?"

I sat for a minute, not sure how much I wanted to say about that. Then I said, "This guy in high school talked me into getting in his car with him, after he'd been drinking. He said he wanted to talk to me about this other girl, that I was friends with. I know I shouldn't have gotten in the car, but he gave me no warning of intending anything like that."

"I guess they don't. You know, the people who do that, they're good at acting like they're just being nice, and everything's fine, until they get you."

"Maybe you're right. I certainly wasn't expecting anything like that. And now, I'm told that I should try to forgive. Not for the guy's sake, but for mine, so the memory of it won't hurt me as much. But I don't think I can."

I took out a tissue and put it up to my eyes, which were suddenly brimming with tears. I put the box up on the table, just in case. "Forgive," said Rick with an exasperated snort, "I'll be damned if I'm gonna forgive that guy. He's a monster."

"Didn't your parents try to get him arrested, or sue the hospital, something like that?" I wanted to know.

"I have no idea, but I don't think so. They just brought me home. My mom cried a lot, but we never really talked about it. Then about six months later, we moved."

He took a long sip of coffee, staring out the window, then fixed his eyes on me and asked, "What about with you? Did you call the police?"

"No," I said, "I didn't want my parents to find out. Anyway, I just wanted to forget about it."

"That's another thing, with people who do that stuff. They know we're not going to tell people. They get away with a lot."

"The guy who did that to me is in jail anyway. At least, I think he still is. He killed a guy," I said.

I was saying this before I later found out that he'd killed a few. "Oh," responded Rick, "well, that's something. You don't have to worry about him showing up again."

"So, nothing like that happened to the guy who did that to you?" I asked him.

"I have no idea, but probably not. But that was in Ohio. I don't worry about running into him. With any luck, he might be in jail. Or dead."

"Well, God willing, at least he's out of your way. I'm sorry, you know, that I yelled at you, earlier. I don't even know why I got so upset."

"It happens," he said, looking at me guardedly, and then glancing out the window.

"You want some more coffee?" I asked him.

"No," he said, "but could you find me some paper, and a pen or something?

"Sure," I said, "are you going to write to your family?"

"No," he said, with another snort of derision, "well, maybe later at some point. But no, not today. I just thought I might try writing a poem, sometime today, or something like that."

"You write poetry?" I asked him, with a relieved smile, so happy for an upbeat change of subject.

"Yes, I do. Been published, too, in a poetry mag at that Booth University, you know, in that town near Possumtown, even though my Dad said the poem probably wasn't good enough. But I started taking a poetry class, sort of an adult-education class, not at the university, but the instructor was a known poet who worked at the university sometimes. He helped me get the poem published. I got a lot more, but my only copies are in my parents' house. If I write one soon, I'll show you."

"I would love to see them," I said, beaming, "I wonder if that's a good way to express how you feel about all the things you've been through."

He looked at me, his eyes suddenly critical, and said, tersely, "Maybe. What about you? You ever try anything like that? Maybe it would help you, and then you wouldn't start screaming when someone touches your shoulder to ask you a question."

I looked back at him and laughed, not sure what to say to that. Thinking for a minute, I carefully responded, "You could be right about that. I used to keep a journal off and on when I was younger, but with nursing school I left it off because I didn't have time."

"You make time," he said, flatly, then he added, "Did you know that Mae West kept a journal? She said, "*Keep a journal, and someday it'll keep you.*"

"Wow, I never heard that. Did she do much writing?"

"Yeah, a lot. She wrote screenplays and plays and all. Just proves that blondes can be writers. You too."

I laughed. "I never even thought about doing that. But hey, if I wanted to try it, how would I even start?"

"Do some reading, that's how. You could even try Rod McKuen. His work is all over the place. People make fun of his poems, but they're pretty good, I think, and easy to read. You know that song *Jean,* from the radio?"

"Oh yeah, like, *Jean, Jean, you're young and alive,*" I laughed a little, and he did too.

"Kind of corny, but pretty good, you have to admit," said Rick, "and I like a lot of his poems. When you think about it, nothing wrong with being popular. I wish the other poets wouldn't pick on him so much. Probably jealous."

"That happens to a lot of sensitive people," I said, adding, "okay, I can probably find one of his books pretty easily. If I try writing something, I'll let you know."

"That's great," he said, with a guarded smile, and then stretched his arms up behind his head, putting his glasses slightly askew, saying, "So, where would some paper and a pen be kept, around here? Father Douglas' office? Should I go over there and get them?"

"No, it's okay, I'm going there anyway, I'll bring you some. Want another cup of coffee, too?"

"Sure, that sounds good. Just black'll be fine. Thanks."

He stretched again, and turned to look out the window. I headed off to get the pen and paper, thinking, *Wow, a poet. Here in Pittsburgh. When do you meet one of those?*

CHAPTER ELEVEN

The Funeral

I FOUND A ROD McKuen book in a local bookstore and was starting to read it, but I didn't get far. I had a lot to do, and the time passed quickly. Then, on the Wednesday before Easter, for the first time in many years, I got a phone call from my friend, Denise. "I've been trying to reach you since last Friday night!" yelled Denise. "When are you ever home?"

"This is the week before Easter," I said, "there's a lot to do at the House."

"All week, though? I swear it's been almost a week I've been trying to reach you," she responded, a bit more calmly.

"I'm sorry, I would have loved to answer your call," I said, completely truthfully. "How long has it been since you actually called me? Since we actually spoke? I call you every Christmas but I'm lucky if I get to talk to your son. He always tells me, Mom's too tired, but I know what that means."

"Donna," she said, "I want to stop drinking. I mean, that was my big news, originally."

"Denise," I said, ecstatically, "that's still big news. It's wonderful. I've been waiting to hear that for forever. What made up your mind?"

"Well, I want to tell you about it, but there's another piece of big news, and it's not good."

Oh, no, I was thinking, and said, "What happened?"

"It's not me, it's Miranda. Sit down for a second, Donna. Are you sitting down?" she insisted.

"Yes," I responded, "this really isn't good, is it?"

"No," said Denise, and started crying, "She's dead, Donna. Some horrible man strangled her right outside her house while her son Rodney watched. And then this whole other thing happened, where John Smith, remember him? He got out of jail."

My heart went to my throat, "Oh, no."

"That's what I thought when I saw him coming out of the A&W. I saw him the same night I decided to stop drinking, the same night Miranda died, last Friday."

"Friday the thirteenth," I said.

"You know, I didn't even notice that," she said. "Anyway, too bad they couldn't put off the service until after Easter, I hope you can still come. It's tomorrow."

"Oh, my God," I almost screamed, "What time? Is the service at the Lutheran Church?"

"Of course. And did you know that John Smith is Rev. Smith's nephew? How's that for weird? I swear I never heard that before, did you?"

"No. Oh, my God, Denise, this is all a little too much for me," I said, reaching in my bag for a cigarette and opening a window, "Don't tell me anymore about John Smith, okay, let's just focus on Miranda."

"Well okay," she said, "but you should prepare yourself, because you're gonna hear some of this tomorrow. I mean, that son of Miranda's, Rodney, he's friends with my Jeff, you know? Anyway, he managed to keep Smith in one place so his wife could run away, but it's a long story, I guess it can wait. But I need to talk to you about not drinking. I wanted to go to a meeting, but I wasn't sure where they were or what to say."

"I'll help you," I said, swinging back to being ecstatic over her quitting booze, "We can go together. There isn't much time, I am guessing I only have a couple of days and will be expected back here on Saturday for the Easter Vigil. That is always a big deal at the House, and there is a big dinner on Easter that they will need help with. But I will still be there Friday, that's a good day to do it. We will find a meeting; we might have to go into town, but it won't be hard. You look up AA in the phone book and call them. Do that tonight after we get off the phone and we'll go on Friday. I'm so glad to hear it, I would do anything to help. But so sad about Miranda. I wonder, if she got a few more days to live and heard your news, whether she would have stopped, too. But it doesn't bear thinking about. Listen, let's get off the phone and you can call AA and I'll call Mom and tell her I'm coming."

The next day dawned gray, a fitting look for Maundy Thursday, as anyone could see by just looking out the window. I went over to the House to help Yves with breakfast and some of the prep for the rest of the day, and as we were cutting vegetables together, I tried to tell him how big all this news really was in my life. "I have been waiting all these years for one of them to stop drinking," I said, "and now one dies and the other stops drinking all on the same night."

"And it's the week before Easter," said Yves. "If you'd been home last weekend you probably would have heard about it at that church that you sometimes go to."

"Well, I would have heard about Miranda dying, anyway," I responded, "and the man who almost killed her son, he went to high school with us too. So, he's back in jail now. I guess he killed the guy who killed her, so he was probably trying to protect her, but I still don't trust him. He might have killed her himself at some later point in time. That son of hers, he must be really brave."

"Yes," said Yves, "but here's what I don't understand. Possumtown is a quiet little place, isn't it? Why is there so much going on there? Don't you find that strange?"

I laughed, "Well, I don't find it strange because I grew up there, and I know that folks there have always had stuff going on, same as folks anywhere. Isn't that true in Jamaica, too? I mean I didn't get a chance to see that movie, *The Harder They Come,* but I have been listening to the soundtrack, and it sounds like some pretty serious stuff goes on over there."

"Yes," said Yves, "well, I didn't see the movie either, but yes, there is a lot going on in Jamaica. Why not? That's life, isn't it? But a quiet life, isn't that what most people want?"

"I don't think I do," I said, "I mean, I wound up working here, and I love it, but it isn't giving me a quiet life or anything."

"Well," said Yves, "at least for now, all we have to do is cut these vegetables."

So we did, until we got the lunch ready to be served, and then I had to say, "I guess I better go now. I don't want to miss the funeral. I've got time, but still, I want to get there early so I can pick up my parents, talk to Miranda's kids, take my time. It's going to be a big thing. Very sad, God knows."

Yves turned and looked at me kindly, saying, "Remember that we will be praying for you, okay? Sometimes it helps just to know that. And do your best to help them, but don't try too hard. We want you back in one piece." He smiled at me, and I smiled back.

"I'll be careful," I said. "Thanks, Yves. Keep an eye on Rick for me, okay?"

On my way back to my apartment, I was thinking about Miranda's kids.

Nothing would take away the pain of losing their mother. Even so, I couldn't stomach facing Miranda's kids without bringing them something. I would stop at the mall outside town before I picked up my parents. For the girl, another Barbie? And something pretty for her hair. She had nice hair, like Miranda's.

There were little boys. Babies, last time I'd seen them. I didn't know how big they were, so clothes were out. Maybe one of those popper toys for the little one, and another book for the bigger one? I got him Pat the Bunny last time, and he seemed to like it. The older ones, I knew their sizes better. Ages ten and thirteen. I would get them sweatshirts. Maybe a little bigger so they could grow into them. Boys that age grow fast. I didn't know how much it would help but it was something I could do, and I needed to do something. I would have plenty of time to think about it more during the drive. I went to my apartment, made a flask of tea for the road, grabbed an apple for a snack, my suitcase that I'd packed last night after getting off the phone with my parents, and I was gone.

I felt better once I was on my way. There wasn't much chance of being late, but even so, I would feel even better when I was there, done with my shopping, picked up my parents, and gone on our way to the church. Once I got to that point, I was feeling an intense mixture of dread and anticipation, so eager to see my old friends and family but so unprepared for the sight of Miranda in a coffin.

Although, as it happened, the coffin was closed. Miranda's body had become so dried out and misshapen from being exposed to the elements for two days, even though she'd been mainly in the backroom of her house, that the funeral home was unable to do much to make her presentable and Rodney, since it was ultimately his choice, opted for a closed coffin. Rev. Smith told him it was a wise choice and would make it easier for his younger brothers and sister, as well. They had placed the coffin on the altar so

Miranda's family and friends could kneel and pray for her next to it. I proceeded to do just that, as soon as I entered the church and signed the book, and after praying and talking with Miranda in my mind, I felt like I'd been in another place and time while I knelt there, finally having the conversation with Miranda I'd been waiting for years to have, but a bit one-sided.

I asked her what to do for her kids. There was no answer, of course, but just asking the question made me feel a little better. I wanted to help Denise too, of course, and was looking forward to going to that meeting with her, but that could wait until evening, or maybe the next day. Now that Denise was sure she wanted to stop drinking, I felt like I could rest easy that it would happen in time, and there was no need to rush it. But the kids, what do they need?

I went to talk to Rodney and was at a loss for words. Fortunately, he was easy to talk to and didn't give me the resistance Miranda used to give me, which I half-expected him to. Instead, he seemed happy to talk with me and eager to hear about the house. "Aunt Donna," he said, "I was hoping you would come. Denise told me how she was having trouble reaching you, I was afraid she wouldn't get to you in time."

"It was close," I said, "but here I am. I am so sorry, Rodney."

"I know," he said, "Thanks for that. Of course, we all miss her so much. It was pretty tough on the little ones, I was hiding it from them at first. Well, hiding it from everybody, because I was afraid of getting sent to foster homes. But did you hear? We are staying at my brother's friend's house, and it looks like we might be able to go on staying there. They're applying for guardianship, and if they get it, we can all stay together. And they're really nice people. So lucky for us. Here, you want to meet them? Oh, they're talking with Rev. Smith right now. You can meet them soon, though."

"Rodney," I said, "I wish I had known that you were managing everything on your own. I'm sure I could have done something to help. I'm so sorry about that. How did you do it?"

"Oh," he said, "well, it's a long story. We'll talk about it some other time. I want to hear about where you work, too. Do you really work in a home for homeless winos? I'm really interested in looking at programs that get people to stop drinking. It must be fascinating."

"Oh, I think it is," I said, and smiled at him.

Of course, he wanted to know about that. He must have been dying to get his mother to stop, just like I had been. Then I said, "Oh my, is that Dan? Wow, he got a lot bigger. Hi, Dan, I am just so glad to see you, sweetie," I continued, and hugged Dan too.

He gave me a big smile, with that big mouth of his, and looked up at me with tears in his eyes. "I am so sorry. You poor kid," I said, pulling a tissue out of my pocketbook and wiping his eyes with it.

"Thanks, Aunt Donna," he said, adding, "You know, I knew she was dead. I was just acting like I didn't to make Rodney feel better."

I wasn't completely sure what he meant by that, but I hugged him again, saying, "You're a good brother. Are you taking care of your sister and the babies, too?"

"Yes, and you know what? They like books all of a sudden. So, we've been looking at books together, and now, I guess I like them too. Except, I'm not up to the books they want me to read in school. But I can read *Pat the Bunny* with them."

"I got another one," I said, "and you can see if you like that one. It's called *Go, Dogs, Go*. Do you like dogs?"

"Yes, I do," said Dan, smiling.

"Then I think you're going to like this book. Another time, maybe we could go to the store and you could pick out a few more that you think you might like. We probably don't have time right now, but sometime soon," I promised, so happy with the idea that they would read more books.

"Yes," said Dan, "if it's okay with Nancy and Al. They are trying to be our guardians. We really want them to be, because they are so nice to us and the food is so good. I never ate so much in my life," he said, looking up at me with an expression of total gratitude.

"I know Nancy and Al," I said with a smile, "and they are wonderful people. I'm so happy to hear that."

"Hey," said Dan, "Here's Nina. She wants to show you that Barbie you gave her last year," he finished with a giggle, and went over to his little sister and two baby brothers, picking up TomTom, the smallest one, and putting him on one of the upholstered chairs. TomTom laughed delightedly at Dan and slid down to the floor so he would do it again, and Dan groaned. A woman standing nearby laughed, "He's going to keep doing that, Dan, don't worry, I'll pick him up. Come here TomTom," she said, picking him up.

I went over to the woman and held out my hand. "Hi, I'm Donna," I said, "I don't remember meeting you, and I thought I knew everybody at the church."

"Well, hello," she said, "I'm Mary. I am so glad to meet you. I've been hearing about you from all these kids, including my daughter Lucy, who talked to you here at church, I believe."

I wilted a little, wondering if Mary was thinking about what I had said to Lucy and her friend, about what happened with John Smith. It crossed my mind, not for the first time, that it might have been better if I hadn't told such a personal story to two young girls. But Mary kept her eye contact and bright smile, showing no signs of making any judgment on my personal history. Hopefully she hadn't heard the whole story. Not that it was my fault that it happened, exactly, but I was always sensitive about other people maybe thinking it was, somehow.

Mary continued, "I am very fond of this church, you know? But I can't sit though the service. Hurts my back."

"I used to love coming here," I said, "but now I work at a Catholic Worker House, for homeless men. I know it sounds yucky, but I never did anything that I found so rewarding."

"That sounds fascinating to me. I hope we can get to know each other better. Maybe I could bring my daughter Lucy up to Pittsburgh for a day and pay you a visit. It would do both of us some good, visiting a place like that. Oh, look at little GG over there. Do you think maybe he needs some attention?"

Mary was still holding TomTom, the younger baby, but little GG, who was more of a toddler, was looking a bit lost, so I walked right up to him, squatted down to his level, and looked in his eyes. He teared up, suddenly, and held out his arms. I picked him right up and he put his arms around my neck, burying his head in my shoulder. I could feel my shoulder getting wet from his tears. "That's okay, GG," I said softly, "that's okay. Everybody feels sad today. Of course."

He just stayed with his head on my shoulder, sobbing gently. He didn't feel that heavy, so I continued standing with him there, and when Rodney saw us, he came over. "Aw," he said, "GG, I shouldn't have left you by yourself so much. Are you okay?"

I looked at him and just shook my head slightly saying, "Don't worry, he is going to be all right, but I think maybe he needs to cry a little," and held GG closely, moving gently from side to side.

Rodney said, "Thanks for helping, Aunt Donna. I just feel bad that I didn't notice him over there for a while. I'm glad you did."

"Hey," I said, "you can't be everywhere. I'm happy to help. How are you holding up, anyway? This has to be difficult for you too."

"Yeah, well, of course, it is," said Rodney, haltingly. "But it's hard for me to feel sad or at least not as sad as I think I should, with so many other things to think about. But the great thing about living with Nancy and Al is that I don't have to worry about the babies quite as much. So, I guess I was getting a little off my guard, 'cause usually I would never forget GG."

"Dan says he is interested in reading now," I said, changing the subject, "That's so great. Is that Nancy's influence too?"

"Actually, it was Wilma that was talking about books all the time," said Rodney, "She's my friend from school who helped me the night Mom died. She got all the young ones, Nina and GG too, going for books. It's okay with me, but I certainly never thought of it. There was too much to think about."

"Wow, you've been through a lot. How great that your friend was there to help you. I'd like to hear more about that sometime, but maybe today wouldn't be the day for that."

"Thanks, Aunt Donna, I appreciate it. I'm trying to keep my eye on all the kids, in here, and it's keeping me busy," he said with a grin.

I might have wanted to hear more about it right away if I had realized that Wilma was Rick's little sister, but I didn't put that together till much later on. I continued, "About the books. I was talking with Dan about going to a bookstore at some point. Would it be okay with you, if I got you kids a few more books?"

He shrugged and said, "Sure, help yourself. The more the merrier. We just have to keep TomTom away from them. He's like one of those moths that eat paper."

Suddenly, GG raised his head slightly and said, "Yes, books. Like books. More?"

I smiled and said, "of course, GG, if you want more books, I'll get them. What sort do you want?"

But his head was buried into my shoulder again. Of course, that was a tough question for a day like today. I could just get a few more and see.

"So, could I talk to Nancy for a minute?" I asked Rodney.

"Sure," he said, "Didn't I introduce you before? I must have forgotten."

"You don't need to," I said with a smile, "We know each other from high school. Nancy's great, I like her a lot. I'm glad I will have an excuse to keep in touch with her better, with you kids living there."

"I bet she likes you too, 'specially since you don't drink," he said with a smile. "That's about all she remembers about Mom and Denise, for sure. She doesn't much like it when people drink a lot."

He smiled kind of wryly. "Still keeps close tabs on her hubby, does she?" I commented.

"Yes," he said quietly, "that she does."

So, that conversation over, we walked across the room to talk to Nancy. I was still holding GG, who seemed to have gone to sleep, so it wasn't hard to get her attention.

"Oh," she said, "what's up with my little GG?"

"He was sad, but now I think he's sleeping it off," I said with a smile. "Best to keep him as he is," I added, since she seemed ready to take him off my hands. She almost gave me a look, but then seemed to think better of it, and smiled, "Well I should thank you, Donna, for giving so much support to this little family over the years, while the rest of us were just oblivious to what they were going through."

"I was oblivious to most of it, too," I said, "and I told Rodney, I wish I had done more. But Miranda didn't seem to want help. I think she didn't want anybody to know how bad things had become."

"Maybe that's right," said Nancy. "I did try to be friends with her in school, but I couldn't understand why she liked to drink so much. She seemed to have a lot of mood swings, too. That could have been from the drinking, or maybe because she was pregnant by the time we all graduated. And Denise too, almost at the same time. Did it ever bother you that they both drank so much?"

"I don't think it bothered me in school so much as afterward. Believe me, I did try to talk both of them into quitting, but there's only so much you can do. Thank God Denise wants to quit, now. I wish Miranda could have gotten to that point."

"Really?" said Nancy, "Denise is thinking of quitting? Now, that is really good news," she smiled, looking genuinely happy to hear it.

"She has already," I said, smiling too, "and you can imagine how happy I was to hear that. She made the decision last Friday, the same night that Miranda died."

"Oh, my God," said Nancy, "I got chills when you said that. One might make it and the other didn't. Is that really God's intention, do you think? It just doesn't seem fair on these kids."

"Not like I can really answer that question, because I wonder about things like that all the time, too. But I guess only God knows the reason things work out the way they do."

"That's right," said Nancy, repeating, "Only God knows."

"Well, one thing I can say for sure is that these kids are lucky to have you and Al," I added.

"Well, thank you," said Nancy with a smile, "of course, we're not guardians yet, but it should happen soon, and we're so grateful."

"Me too," I agreed. Then I was wondering, "Wow, is that a policeman over there? He looks kind of familiar somehow."

"Oh, yeah," said Nancy, "that's the policeman who came when John Smith was attacking those poor kids, last week. Wow, maybe he just got here. It's nice that he's showing up for poor Miranda. I forgot his name, but we know his face, because he works in Possumtown. That's probably why he looks familiar to you."

"Oh, right," I said, taking in the forty-something man with a sparse cover of light brown hair, blue eyes and a quiet but watchful expression.

Rodney saw him and went over, eyes shining. I sort of sidled over toward them, curious about what Rodney would say to him. "Hi, Ed," said Rodney, "I'm so glad you came. I know you have a lot to do. Really appreciate it."

"Well," said the policeman, "I wanted to see how you were doing. How is it, where you're living? Are you doing all right with Nancy and Al?"

"They have been wonderful, and Dan tells everyone how much we all want them to be our guardians."

"You feel that way too?" asked the policeman. "I mean, you feel like you can live in that home until you're eighteen without going crazy?"

Rodney looked over at me and we both laughed, then looked around to make sure Nancy wasn't listening. "Ed," he said to the policeman, "This is my Aunt Donna. She was a good friend of my Mom's. It's okay to talk in front of her," he added with a grin, continuing, "well, Nancy and Al have their moments, but they are doing their best with the five of us, I think. Nancy is so good with the babies, it's such a load off my mind. Nina is just happy being with me, Dan and the babies, as long as she still can watch her TV shows, and she loves Nancy's cooking, though probably not as much as Dan does. She's still more attached to me than to anyone else and it really hasn't been that long. But Nancy does make a fuss about dressing Nina up, along with her own daughter, and Nina loves going to church in her pretty outfits. So, I think she will warm up."

"All right," said Ed, the policeman. "That all sounds good. Let me know if anything changes."

"I will, but I think things are okay," said Rodney.

I suddenly remembered where I had seen Ed before. "Aren't you the policeman who came to our fifth high-school reunion to help me find my lost pocketbook?" I asked him with a smile.

"Oh," said the policeman, "yes, I remember that. And you called and left me a message that your friend had it. That was thoughtful of you, saved me a lot of trouble."

"Well, of course I had to let you know. That was my last reunion, maybe for good, by the way," I added. "So much drinking and craziness, I would rather not have to deal with that again."

"I don't like them myself," said Ed, "it's a drag when people keep asking about my ex."

"Is that because you're divorced? Wow, I can see how that would be difficult," I said, feeling a little awkward all of a sudden.

It seemed like he did too, and almost beat a retreat, saying, "Well, as long as Rodney's okay."

But I had to ask, "You know, I think we talked at the reunion, about how you came to the A&W that time. So, this is actually the third time I'm meeting you."

He blushed, visibly, making me wish I hadn't said that, but then he said, "Yes, I remember that, too."

"Well, thank you for helping Rodney the way you did. Seems like he and I both owe you our thanks. We could use your help out in Pittsburgh."

"You live there? Wow, that's interesting. You know, I worked there the first few years after my training. So exciting in Pittsburgh. I haven't been there in years. What do you do there?"

Rodney piped up, "She works at a home for homeless winos, how about that?"

Ed looked impressed, asking me, "Does he mean the Catholic Worker House? Wow, that place is famous. That must be some interesting job."

"Yes, it is, I love it, although it can be challenging at times," I said.

"Listen," said Ed, "I don't mean to be pushy, but let me make a suggestion. If you ever run into any trouble up there, you should feel free to call me at the station and ask for some help, even if you just want to talk about something. Some homeless guys can be a handful, I've dealt with quite a few in my time," he said, looking at me intently.

"Thank you," I said, "well, that's kind of you. I can't think of anything that we need help with right now, but you never know. Anyway, you are welcome to visit us at the Catholic Worker House, any time," I finished with a smile.

"Hey, you guys," said Rodney, looking a little embarrassed, "I hate to interrupt, but I think Rev. Smith wants to have the service now."

I smiled at my new friend Ed, the policeman, and went to take my seat for the service. *Great,* I was thinking, *it could indeed help a lot to know a nice policeman. And, I almost hate to admit it, but Karen was right about one thing when we saw him at the A&W. He is kind of cute.*

First Meeting

THAT THURSDAY NIGHT, NOT long after the funeral, Denise and I went to an AA meeting. She was told she had to wait until the weekend for an open meeting if she wanted to bring me, but I told her I would be happy to pretend to be a drunk if that's what it took, and to just find a meeting and let's go. There were no meetings in Possumtown, so we settled on one that was in the middle of our trusty nearby little university town, (Booth, the private university that no Possumtown resident could afford), at 7:30. Denise asked me to meet her at a restaurant she knew of, to get something to eat first. Then we both left. I went home to drop off my parents and told them not to worry about my dinner. She took Jeff home to get him something to eat and make sure he was okay, settled in front of the television or on the phone with his friend Rodney.

We met up at 6:30, and I recognized the restaurant as one that I went to with my Dad when I was sixteen, the day we went to the DMV to get my learner's permit. It still had the same dark wooden paneling on the walls and dark red upholstery on the chairs and booths. There was no overhead lighting in the dining area, just lamps placed here and there among the tables, to make us comfortable I guess, but to me it felt dark and creepy. We sat on either side of a small booth and ordered coffee. Denise was so nervous that she couldn't really calm down. "I think I'm going to get a hamburger," she said, "how about you?"

"Probably a Greek salad. Are you okay? You look so nervous," I said, giggling.

"Well, aren't you?" asked Denise, widening her big dark eyes at me.

"Yeah, I guess I am. I've never been to one of these meetings before."

"It does relate to your job, right?" Denise observed, "So, you will learn something useful, maybe."

"I guess I will learn a lot. But honestly, I would go anywhere to help you stop drinking."

She shook her head. "Don't keep saying that. I really appreciate that you're coming with me, but ultimately, I need to do this on my own. And I will be on my own, anyway, after tomorrow. But I am so glad you're coming tonight. I don't know if I could go by myself, I really don't."

"What's your biggest worry about it?" I asked her, going into my nurse role.

"Well, running into someone we know, of course. But I wouldn't let that stop me, don't worry. I just don't want to look stupid, like putting my foot right in my mouth."

"I don't think they would expect you to get it all right off the bat. It isn't like a class, where you get a grade. And people keep going for years, I hope you don't mind me saying that, but that's what I've heard."

"I don't care how long it takes, I just really want to do this. All I put Jeff through." She looked at me with tears in her eyes.

"How did you come to decide to quit?" I had to ask.

"I can't really explain it. It just hit me, that Friday night, like I was telling you on the phone, when I was at this bar over past the college from here, it's been one of my favorites. They have live music Fridays, and all the cute young people show up. I knew a bunch of people there, but suddenly I just wasn't that excited about it, you know. And in the bathroom, some girl was throwing up in one of the toilets, and I looked in the mirror to fix my makeup, and suddenly I just knew I didn't want to do this anymore. I didn't even go back to my seat, I just left. And then on the way home I saw John pulling out of the A&W, and it scared me half to death. Even so, can you believe it, I almost waved to him. That awful man. Why?"

"Well, he did mean a lot to you, at one time. But you didn't, I hope?"

"No, thank God, this time I didn't. I just kept driving, like I didn't even see him. And I got home to Jeff and told him I was going to stop, and he was so happy. So, we made some popcorn," she finished with a smile. "It was so nice, sitting with him, watching television, not drunk. Like years ago, when we used to have fun together."

"I'm so glad," I said, tears coming to my eyes too. "So, Jeff was okay with you going tonight?"

"He wanted to come," she said, almost sobbing again.

"Now don't make your mascara run. He'll be fine, I'm just so happy for what this will do for you. No more losing it over the first stupid man who looks at you. No more driving drunk. No more hangovers," I finished, stroking her hair back from her face.

She looked at me and managed a smile, blowing her nose on a napkin. "That really is great, by the way. I already noticed that. No splitting headache when I wake up in the morning. It feels really good."

Our food came. Denise didn't really eat much of her hamburger, and I was eyeing it jealously around my boring salad. "Can I have some of your fries?" I asked her.

"Sure," she said, "but I thought you were trying to watch your weight?"

I shrugged. "A few won't hurt. This salad is boring. The feta cheese is so salty, I don't think it's supposed to taste like that."

"Send it back," she said.

"No, I couldn't. I serve food at the House, you know. It's not an easy job."

"I'll send it back. Hey," she said, turning around and waving to the waiter with a big smile on her face. He came over, all smiles, and she said, still smiling, "Could you do us a big favor and take back my friend's salad? The feta cheese is kind of hard and weird-tasting."

He took it with a sigh and said he would see what he could do. "Bring her back a hamburger with fries, like mine," she added, with a big smile with teeth.

A few minutes later I had my burger and it tasted great. "God, Denise, thank you so much. This really hits the spot. Somehow, after this long day, and the funeral, I just needed something more than a salad."

Her face crumpled. "The funeral was so sad," she gasped between sobs. "Those poor kids."

"I know," I said, and handed her a clean napkin. "But you know, just think how happy Miranda would be to know that you stopped drinking."

"I wish she was here with us. God, I wish it, Donna. I wasted all those years not even talking to her, over that stupid, horrible man." She burst into sobs again.

I stroked her hair again. "Try not to blame yourself for that," I said. "She didn't call you, either. I think it was the alcohol, working on both of you. There's nothing you can do now, except take care of yourself, and I know that's what she would want you to do."

She eventually blew her nose again, and then looked at me and took my hand. "Donna, I'm sorry that I keep talking about John Smith. After what he did to you. I should have known right from then to stay away from him."

I looked away from her, not sure I could manage talking about that. Finally, I said, smiling, "Well, just don't say his name a third time, or he might show up and kill us all. Isn't that from some old story or something?"

"What?" she gasped, laughing through her tears.

"The cook, Yves, over at the House, was talking about some old story like that. You'll have to come up and see the place, meet those people. You would love Yves, he's so funny. But he's married, so hands off."

"Hey, I'm gonna be sober now, so you won't have to say that every time," she said, laughing again.

"Seriously though, did you get to talk much to Nancy and Al? I know you weren't crazy about them in high school, but they seem to be doing great with those kids."

"I did used to talk to them sometimes in high school, but not really since then. They were kind of quiet, I thought."

"Right," I said, "I was friends with Nancy for a while, especially while you were away in Philadelphia. She used to tell me to tell you and Miranda to stop drinking."

"It seemed like Nancy wanted to be friends with Miranda, but I guess the drinking put her off. Probably didn't appreciate my drinking, either. She gave me kind of a funny look when she saw me today, so I guess she remembers me," Denise giggled.

"As long as the kids are okay. I have to say, they already look better than they did last summer at their stepfather's funeral. Good food and a nice clean home, makes a lot of difference, I guess."

"Poor Miranda, she won't get to watch them grow up," Denise blew her nose again. "I'm not letting that happen to me and my son."

I was finishing my burger. "Probably I shouldn't eat all of these fries," I commented, laughing a little. "Why don't you go in the bathroom and fix yourself up, and I'll settle this."

"Oh, you don't have to do that, Donna, I was going to treat you," she said, wiping her eyes.

"My treat this time, and you can do it next time. Maybe tomorrow, if it works out. Go ahead now, so we can get going."

The meeting was in an office building, a nice older building made of stone, with an impressive staircase, like many of the buildings there, and we walked to the side of the building to a courtyard in the back where there was an AA sign hanging from a doorway. When we went inside, the room was pleasant with upholstered chairs and a polished wooden table. There was a desk against the back wall with a metal rack holding pamphlets and some books, and a small cardboard sign on the table that said something about anonymity. And in the spirit of that, I won't describe the meeting except to say that Donna was pleased with all the attention she got for being new, and she didn't flirt too much, which was good because it was suggested not to do that.

We both got meeting lists and agreed to go to another one the next day. I gave her a big hug for being so brave, and headed home. I spent most of the next day with my parents. They let me nap and my Mom made her delicious roast chicken and home-grown vegetables for lunch. Denise and I went to another meeting in the afternoon that had more people than the first one, and some of the folks had stories that were sad and disturbing. Fortunately, Denise seemed unfazed by this, saying that she wasn't that surprised and actually felt good about the idea that she didn't have the worst story around. I left her in good spirits, and felt my spirits lifting, too.

••• CHAPTER THIRTEEN •••

New Guy

TIRED AS I WAS after the long drive from home, I couldn't wait to get back to the Catholic Worker House. I hadn't read much of the Rod McKuen book yet, just a few poems here and there as I scanned through it at night before I fell asleep. But, during the drive back, I could feel the beginnings of a poem, or something to write, percolating through my mind. It would be about Miranda, of course, and Denise, and me, the irony of Miranda's death on the same night as Denise's sudden leap into life-saving sobriety. The huge, gaping abyss of the pain of Miranda's suffering, which I could only guess at, and her bereft children.

When I got home, I followed a suggestion from Rick and once I was settled in with a can of Tab in my living room, I just sat and wrote out everything that popped into my mind about the whole situation. I went to sleep with my brain full of what I wrote, and in the morning, over coffee, I wrote out a first draft of a poem, or a poem-like writing. "It doesn't matter," Rick had said, "just get some stuff written down and it'll take shape over time."

I was so pleased to have this first draft to show him, and when I got to the House I bustled back to the kitchen, figuring Rick would probably be there drinking coffee. I saw Yves, who was cleaning up after breakfast, and said, "Hey, young lady, I could've used some help around here," with a phony frown.

Then laughing, he held out his arms for a hug. His hugs always felt safe and warm, good medicine for a traumatized waif like me. "Oh, Yves," I said, tears coming to my eyes, "It was so sad. Her poor kids that she left behind."

"I'm sorry to hear it," he said, releasing me with a sad smile, "but it's good to have you back. There's been a few changes, even in this short amount of time."

"Where's Rick?" I asked him, "I wonder why he's not here drinking his coffee like usual. Believe it or not, I actually made a rough draft of a poem and I'm dying to show him."

"Oh, that's wonderful," said Yves with another smile, "I would love to see it, if you don't mind showing me. But I'm afraid I have bad news about Rick. Well, bad for us, but maybe good for him. His family found some kind of sheltered work program for him, close to where they live. He might get his own apartment, even have a car. He was all excited about it."

Hearing this, my heart sank. "Wow," I said, "I guess I should be happy for him, but I can't help feeling disappointed. I was looking forward to seeing him. Don't you think it was great, having him here? Our own poet, that was something."

"He is certainly an interesting character. He did leave his parents' phone number I think, but you'd have to ask Father Douglas."

"I still wonder about that family of his, and I'm not sure I'd be comfortable about calling them. But I'll think about it."

"Well, you'd have to do it soon, because he said they were moving to England. I guess his Dad got a job transfer to work in Europe."

"Oh yeah, Rick was telling me about that. I have to say, I don't like it. It's not good for Rick. I mean, even if this work program goes well, he's going to need their support. Why on earth are they doing this?"

"God knows. Father Douglas did tell him that he could always come back. So, he has us, if nothing else."

"Can I sit down for a minute?" I had to sit, feeling light-headed all of a sudden, and added, "I'm having trouble dealing with this. I know I'm going to be worrying about him, but I don't think calling his family would help. I mean, they don't even know me, so they're not exactly likely to listen to me if I tell them not to move to England."

"He said his father was already leaving, probably has left by now, so don't waste your time telling them that. Father Douglas says we should pray for them, and Rick. Maybe that's all we can really do for Rick right now," said Yves.

"Wow," I said, as Yves handed me a cup of coffee.

I poured some milk into it and stirred in a spoon of sugar, thinking about that first time I had coffee with Rick, after he'd surprised me in the Chapel. "He wasn't even here that long, only maybe three or four months, but I sure will miss him."

"We all will. Meanwhile, a new guy showed up, like, the day after Rick left."

"Really, well that's something," I said, "at least it will keep things interesting around here."

Yves shook his head slightly. "I don't know what to make of this one. I'm a little worried that he might be bad news. Keeping my eye on him."

"What's his name?" I asked.

"Dave, something. Forgot his last name. He's from Ohio. Really big, blond guy with one of those military buzz cuts and really strange eyes, like a really dark blue or something. Real tough guy, you never see him smile. I don't know, he just gives me the creeps."

"That doesn't sound good. I don't think I've ever heard you describe one of the men that way. Well, I guess I'll get a look at him at lunch. I'm gonna go say hi to Father Douglas. You need my help with lunch?"

"Just cutting vegetables for the salad. That would be a big help, if you don't mind," said Yves.

"Same old thing," I said, laughing, "you don't like chopping vegetables much, do you, Yves?"

He smiled and said, "Hey, you know, it gets monotonous. You wouldn't believe how much time I spend chopping vegetables, just, say, carrots, celery, onions, stuff like that. I don't really mind that much, but if you're willing to help, I'll take it. Anyway, it goes faster when you have company."

"Okay, I get it. Of course, I'll help you. Let me talk to Father Douglas first, in case he needs me for something."

I finished my coffee and went back down the hall to Father Douglas' office. He was there, and in front of his desk sat a man who matched Yves' description of the new guy. His face was chiseled, like a sculpture, and was set in a grim expression that was almost a scowl, but not quite. Father Douglas was looking at the man over his glasses. His tall slim build was probably not much more than half the size of this man, yet he seemed completely calm, facing him. I knew I couldn't do that, but seeing his calm demeanor gave me the nerve to at least say, "Hi."

I waved to Father Douglas, and he smiled over the new guy's head. "Donna, I want you to meet Dave. He got here yesterday. Could you sit down and help him finish his intake form, while I work on something else? I'm trying to get some more food organized. We have enough for right now, but we can always use more, of course, especially since we have been getting some more men in here recently. And I want to finish it before the mail goes out at one o'clock."

"Okay, Father Douglas," I said, pulling another chair up toward the desk, but not too close to the new guy.

His size was intimidating to me, and even a few feet away, I could smell the sweat and the sheer, contracted muscular intensity of the man. I tried to smile, and said, "Hi, Dave."

Feeling my throat closing up from anxiety, I continued anyway. "Let's see how far you got with the intake form," I croaked, as I picked the paper up. I sensed him looking at me, but I didn't look up, yet. He was silent.

I glanced at the form and said, "Okay, I see where we didn't yet get the address of the last place you were living,"

"My parents' house," he finally said, in a voice that wasn't as deep as I expected, and raspy, probably from cigarette smoke, "291 Livingston Avenue, Kettering, Ohio."

I finally looked up, and I was struck by his eyes. Was I right in thinking he had more than one pupil? I had to ask him, "Your eyes are so unusual. Do you have any difficulty seeing? I mean, do you wear glasses sometimes?"

He looked away, and said gruffly, "I have astigmatism, that's all. I used to have glasses, but I don't really need them. I see all right."

"So, Kettering," I asked, trying to change the subject, "where is that?"

"Not far from Dayton," he said, his face relaxing into a half-smile that was almost a leer.

"Too bad you didn't meet this other guy who was here, he was from Dayton too," I started, but Father Douglas interrupted me.

"Donna, we don't discuss information like that," he said.

I blurted, "Oh, sorry, Father, that's right, I'm sorry I forgot."

Father Douglas just looked at me for half a minute and calmly said, "Don't worry, just keep it in mind from now on," and went back to his letter.

I glanced back to Dave, who looked vaguely embarrassed. "Okay, Dave," I asked him, "can I get your parents' phone number?" and we got back to the form, finishing it up in just a few minutes.

I put it on Father Douglas' desk, and asked Dave, "I guess you already know your way around the place. You want a cup of coffee or something?"

"No, thanks," he said, quietly, in that raspy voice of his, "I'll just head over to the TV room and see if the news is on."

The TV room was just across the hall from Father Douglas' office, on the front left of the first floor, with the chapel behind it, on the left in the back of the building. They were separated by the storage closet, which was the territory of Grace, the cleaning lady. Dave slouched off to the door and then turned and caught my eye. "That guy from Dayton," he said, "you let me know if he comes back, okay?"

"Well," I responded in surprise, "I'm not sure that I can. Seems like I wasn't supposed to mention it. But there's plenty of good guys for you to talk to, around here."

He just looked at me, his gaze turned sarcastic, and sort of snickered, "Sure."

I watched him leave, thinking, *okay, now I get what Yves was talking about.*

CHAPTER FOURTEEN

A Lucky Catch

THE WEEK AFTER EASTER, I got a call from Penny that she wanted to come and visit the House. "I want to talk to you about this class I'm taking, it's really hard," she said, no surprise to me because most of nursing school was like that.

"What might really help me out, is doing my field work at your Worker House," she said, "it ought to be really interesting and my report will help me get a better grade, I hope. This professor is hard to impress, I usually get good grades but now I'm kind of worried."

"I had so many classes like that," I said with a chuckle, "don't worry too much, you'll get through it all right. But you're right about doing the field work at the House, it will make a good field study. I wish I knew about it when I was in school."

"When can I start?" she wanted to know.

"If you have time tomorrow, come on over and meet Father Douglas. Then the three of us can talk over what your schedule will be."

"Probably just a couple of days would do it. I have classes on Monday, Wednesday and Friday afternoons, so I was thinking Tuesday and Thursday, but only if it works for you guys."

"I don't know of any reason why not, but we just have to check with Father Douglas. I'm looking forward to seeing you. Why don't you come over at 11:00 and if you want, you could stick around and help with lunch, and then have lunch with me and Yves, the cook, after it's finished."

"That sounds great," she said.

And the next day at 11:00, there she was, looking radiant with her scrubbed face and blonde ponytail, wearing jeans and a bulky sweatshirt. "Am I dressed right?" she asked me nervously, "I know these clothes are really informal, but I didn't think I should dress up. Will this be okay, that I'm wearing jeans?"

"Sure," I said, "you look just fine. You were right about not dressing up, I forgot to talk to you about it, but I think you got it just right. It would be a little much for some of these guys to see a pretty young lady in a dress running around."

"That's what I figured," she said, nodding.

"Come in the office and meet Father Douglas," I said, and we went through the waiting room and knocked.

Father Douglas was happy to meet Penny, and the whole idea of having a nursing student doing field work at the House really appealed to him. "I think it's wonderful that a nursing student would come here and learn about our House and the men that live here. Donna will be able to show you around, and you can work with her. That will give you all the experience you need. I hope you will let me know how your class responds to your report. It would be great to have more of a connection with that school."

"I'm sure they'll love hearing about it, I know that I thought it sounded fascinating when Donna told me about it. I'm so glad to be able to do this," Penny said, looking flushed with excitement.

We left the office to introduce her to Yves, both of us so happy with how things were going, and then coming down the hall toward us was Dave. He slowed down as he approached us and stopped right in front of us, so we could not walk around him. "Is this young lady new around here?" he asked us, with a leering expression that made my stomach lurch.

Penny looked at him, eyes wide as a deer in head-lights. "Excuse me, Dave," I said, "but my friend is just visiting. We're on our way to the kitchen. Do you mind?"

He was only looking at Penny, and seemed not to hear me at first, but when I moved to walk by him, he stepped aside, turning and saying to our backs, "Well, nice to meet you, anyway. I'm gonna make sure I get to see you again."

I didn't look at him, but I could feel Penny turning her head to stare at him in shock. Most likely he was still leering. I pulled her into the kitchen and said,

"Yves, could you put on some more coffee, please? My friend Penny and I need to sit down a minute."

Penny looked like she was in a cold sweat. "Who was that?" she asked, her voice high and squeaky.

"That was a new guy named Dave," I said, looking meaningfully at Yves.

Yves just quietly shook his head while he got the coffee started. "I mean," said Penny, "that made me uncomfortable. Wow, Donna, does he have that effect on you? I mean, is that how these guys act around here? I don't know …."

"He's only been here a few days, but no, I can tell you, the guys do not act like that, not most of them. I mean, all the time I've been here, that was the first time I ever saw anything like that. I'll talk with Father Douglas and he will speak with Dave about it. We can't have him acting like that, with you here trying to do your field work, poor kid."

Yves put cups and saucers down on the kitchen table where we were sitting, and said, "That young man hasn't even been here that long and he's already making problems. I'm certainly sorry he made you uncomfortable, miss. You can always come here and sit in the kitchen because he wouldn't dare act like that in here."

"Certainly not," I said, "or anywhere else, once Father Douglas speaks to him about it. I am so sorry, Penny."

"I'll be okay," she said, looking a little calmer, "he just surprised me, that's all. But I'll be all right. I have to learn to deal with all kinds of situations for when I get out in the workforce, right? That's the reality of life today, women have to learn to be tough, don't we, Donna?"

"Sure, but you shouldn't have problems like that here in our House. We'll do something about it, don't worry. I'm glad you're okay," I added, hoping that was true, because I knew that with what Penny went through back in her runaway days, Dave's behavior would have to be a challenge for her.

But that was just the beginning. Even after Father Douglas spoke to him, and then spoke to him again, Dave gave Penny the same weird leering gaze every time he saw her, and he made a point of seeing her often. This went on for weeks. If I remember right, her assignment was for six weeks, and we were in the fifth week when we were working in the kitchen helping Yves, and I realized I forgot to ask Father Douglas whether he had any paperwork he needed help with that afternoon. I went down the hall to see Father Douglas, and Penny came with me to use the bathroom on the hall. Father Douglas and I only spoke for a few minutes, and I was coming back down the hall when I saw Dave lurking near the bathroom where Penny was. He had his back to me when the door opened, and Penny tried to come out. Dave grabbed the door and tried to muscle his way into the bathroom with her, but he didn't notice me coming up behind him. I got there just in time to kick the door shut in front of him and yelled at the top of my lungs, "Oh, no, you don't."

He jumped back, startled, but then got an ugly look on his face and probably would have flattened me if Father Douglas hadn't sprung out of the door to the office behind me. I could see Dave's face going blank when he saw that, and what he didn't see probably would have scared him even more, because Yves was coming out of the kitchen door at about the same time, behind him. I had never seen Yves look more serious than he did on that day, and he and Father Douglas both looked even more grim when Penny quietly emerged from the bathroom. "I hope," said Father Douglas, "that this isn't what it looks like. If it is, young man, I will have to ask you to leave this facility."

That was music to my ears, but it didn't work out that way. Dave cried out in a strangely high-pitched voice, "It was a mistake, I swear. Please don't kick me out, I got no place to go, I'm being honest here."

And in the end, with Dave sent to his room and after a discussion between Father Douglas, Penny and myself, it came about that he would stay after all, provided that he really did change his behavior toward Penny. Father Douglas was set on forcing Dave out, especially after he heard my description of what happened and how it nearly could have been much worse. But Penny, after her initial shock wore off, said she really didn't want Dave to lose his place in the house on her account. "I only have one more week," she said, "maybe I'll just come in next Tuesday and finish up. That should be okay, as long as I stick close to Donna and Yves."

"I don't know," said Father Douglas after giving it some thought, "seems to me that this is exactly the sort of behavior that shouldn't be tolerated here. We've kicked men out just for drinking in their rooms, and this is so much worse than that."

But it wound up exactly as Penny suggested, with her last day the following Tuesday, and she worked with me and Yves in the kitchen almost the entire day.

We did pass Dave in the hall once, and he pointedly didn't even glance at Penny, but he gave me a mean glare that I only just noticed in passing. I really didn't care, as long as Penny was all right, and she seemed fine. But when we talked about it later, she told me how she really felt. "That man is a monster, I am not kidding you, Donna. Look out for him. I don't like the idea of him being here where you're working, and I'm going to call you every weekend and make sure you're okay."

CHAPTER FIFTEEN

Not a Coincidence

AFTER THAT, NOTHING MUCH happened for a few months, and time slipped into summer, with the heat and humidity that's typical for Pennsylvania. At the House, we had air conditioning only on the first floor, so if it was really hot, we let the men bring their mattresses down and sleep in the TV room or cafeteria.

Most of the other men were easy to get along with, and I don't remember any problems, except that once in a while I would notice Dave talking to a few of the other men, and they would usually wind up looking kind of sad or uncomfortable. I was at the point of asking one of these guys if something was going on until I ran into Dave in the hall on my way to the kitchen.

I asked him if he wanted to get a cup of coffee, and he said no, so then I asked him, "Sometimes I notice you talking to some of the guys, and you look kind of annoyed or something. Is everything all right?"

"Sure, it is," he said, with just an edge of sarcasm.

"You're okay? Not unhappy about something?"

"No," he said quietly, "do you have a problem with me?"

I felt pretty awkward by now, but I kept going, "It's just that you look kind of unhappy with things sometimes. So, I wondered if there was a problem we should know about."

"No," he said, with a leering grin, "I'm just fine, thanks."

"Okay," I said, and left him in the hall, feeling like that could have gone better.

I went to the kitchen to help Yves with the vegetables for lunch, and when I saw Yves, I said, "Yves, I need to talk to you."

Yves shushed me, and silently pointed to the dining room. There was Rick, sitting at a table with his back to us, looking out the window. "Wow, I wish I knew he was coming, I would've brought my poem."

"Take it easy with him," said Yves quietly, "he's in a bit of a mood."

I looked at Yves, wondering how bad that might be, and I went into the dining room, walking around to the front of the table so I could see Rick's face. It took him half a minute to register that I was there. Then he jumped a little and said, "Donna," in a strangled-sounding voice.

"Of course, it's me," I said, smiling, "I do still work here, you know."

I wanted to hug him, but I had a feeling that I'd better not. He looked happy to see me, but distant and a little sad. "Hey," I said, "I was looking for you when I got back from that funeral, back around Easter time, but you were gone. I wrote a poem about my friend who died, and I wanted to show it to you. Can I bring it tomorrow? Is something wrong?"

His face was suddenly constricted, almost as if he was trying not to cry. He looked away for a second, then when he looked back, his expression was flat, almost deadpan. "Sure," he said, "I'll look at it. Glad to."

"Well," I said, "it's great to see you again. I was a little worried about you, especially when I heard your family went to England. What happened with that program they found for you? That didn't work out?"

"Not anymore," he said flatly, and got up. "Listen, I gotta go out for a smoke. It's good to see you, Donna," but the brusque tone he used made me feel again like something was wrong that he wasn't telling me about.

"Okay, Rick," I said, "but listen, if there's something bothering you, you can always talk to me or Father Douglas about it."

He turned and said, "Sure," but he kept walking.

I took his coffee cup back into the kitchen and put it into the sink, shrugging at Yves. "Something's going on with him, for sure," I said, "I'd love to know what it is."

"When he came in and asked for coffee," said Yves, "he looked like he'd seen a ghost. I tried to ask him about it, but he just insisted that everything was fine, just like he was doing right now."

"Well," I said, "maybe we'll find out later."

But there was no later. Rick didn't show up for dinner, and when we looked around for him, Yves found that his bag was gone from his room. "Do you think he left?" he asked me, and I said, "Wouldn't he have told us?"

When I asked Father Douglas if Rick had said anything to him, he said no, but he also said quietly, "I could tell something was wrong, but I couldn't help him if he wouldn't tell me what it was. We'll just have to wait and see if he comes back."

Still, I felt sad that he didn't have his dinner, and it didn't help that Dave was walking around with one of his horrible leering grins on his face. I kept wondering if Rick's leaving had something to do with Dave, but I didn't want to ask Dave about it until I knew more.

When I left for home, there was a heavy moon up in the still warm sky. I got to my apartment and turned on all my fans and opened the windows, but it was still hot. I wanted ice cream, and there was none left in the freezer, so I went out to get some, my summer bag, a beige crochet saddle bag with a long crochet strap, hanging by my side. The way to the store was pretty well lit, but I liked to walk along the park, where it was cooler. A figure of a man lurched out toward me, and I grabbed the top of my bag and backed up. Then I registered that the pale, bobbing face was Rick's.

"Rick," I said, "what are you doing here? We looked all over for you. Why did you leave?"

He shook his head, and his face contorted like he was on the verge of tears again. "I can't tell you," he said, and flopped himself down on a nearby bench, leaning over and putting his face in his hands.

I walked over and tentatively sat down next to him. He sat up suddenly and reared back, almost shouting, "I can't believe it. How did that guy wind up here? How did he know where I was?"

"What guy?" I asked.

"That, that … his name's Dave. I just can't believe it," he said again, leaning down and putting his face back in his hands.

"Oh, no," I said, not wanting to believe it myself, "is he the guy who …."

"Who raped me, yes. Yes, yes, he is. I never thought I'd have to deal with him again. And here he is! You know what this means? I may never be rid of him. What can I do about it, if he wants to follow me like that?"

"Don't you think it was probably coincidence? He wouldn't have been actually following you," I said.

"He told me he was looking for me," he said, in a sort of strangled moan, "he for sure is following me, no doubt about it. And I can't think of anything I can do to stop him."

"Well," I said, breathlessly, "you can go to the police, that's what you can do. I'll go with you. This could be a real opportunity, to make him pay for what he did. Let's go."

"No, no, no," he said, almost crying again, "I can't go to the police. They wouldn't listen to me. A guy like me, are you kidding? They'd probably laugh in my face."

"But I'll go with you. We can get Father Douglas to come, if you want. They'll listen to us."

"No, you don't get it. The police despise guys like me. If I asked them for help, they might even beat me up. That's what they do, to guys like me. It's no use."

"Well, please at least come back, and we can talk to Father Douglas about it. Where are you going to sleep? You can't sleep out here. You want me to drive you back to the House? Well, no, I guess you don't want to go back there right now. Tell you what, you can sleep on my couch. That'll be fine. Come on back to my place with me, and I'll make some coffee, and we can go talk to Father Douglas in the morning."

"No," he said, "I can't do that. Listen, I appreciate it, but I'll be okay. It's warm, I've done it before, just let me go."

"Well, if that's what you have to do, but please come back to the House tomorrow, so we can go talk to Father Douglas. Here," I handed him ten dollars, "I know you missed dinner."

"Thanks," he said, taking the ten dollars, "but I think it's best if I don't ever go back to that place again. But thanks, though, really," he said, lurching off the bench and staggering back into the park.

"You be careful," I called after him, "and come on back tomorrow, okay?" but there was no reply.

I sat on the bench in a stupor, and then began to cry. Poor Rick. I had totally forgotten about ice cream, and didn't have any more cash in my bag, so I made my way home, still crying, holding a soggy tissue in front of my face. When I got to my apartment, I grabbed a can of Tab out of the fridge and sat by the front window of the living room, smoking. *By God,* I was thinking, *I am absolutely going to make that man Dave pay for what he did. Doesn't matter what Rick says. I have to do something. But what?*

CHAPTER SIXTEEN

Do Something

AS SOON AS I got to the House, the next morning, I went into Father Douglas' office to talk to him, but he wasn't there. So, I went around to the kitchen, where Yves was still working on getting breakfast for the men. "You gonna help me serve this food today, young lady?" he asked me with a smile, and I just stared at him.

"Oh, Yves," I said, "I don't even want to tell you what happened last night. Rick showed up over by the park, and I talked to him, but he wouldn't come back here, and, well, I guess I should tell Father Douglas. Is he around?"

"He was here, he grabbed some toast and coffee and left. He said he had to go somewhere, I'm not sure what for. Hang around and help me and maybe he'll be back when we're finished."

"Okay," I said, slowly, trying to get clear on whether that would work, "sure, I have to wait for him anyway, so I might as well help out."

"Thanks for your enthusiasm," said Yves, wryly. "Hey, that oatmeal has been simmering for a while now, could you give it a stir?"

"Sure," I said, hoping he wouldn't ask about Rick. I tried to keep my mind on what I was doing, but I kept worrying about Rick, and I was bursting to talk with Father Douglas about it.

When the men came in, I couldn't help looking to see whether Dave was there. Finally, there he was, with two or three guys who looked kind of cowed or almost embarrassed, trailing along behind him almost in spite of themselves. He still had a sort of a sneer on his face, much like the other day. When I looked at him, I felt sick to my stomach. I wanted to yell at him so bad, I was almost trembling with rage. But this wasn't the right time. I wanted to talk to Father Douglas first, and then maybe I would know what to say to Dave.

As we were cleaning up, putting the dishes away and beginning to wipe down the tables, we heard the familiar noise that told us that Father Douglas was back. He had a distinctive loping gait and a way of almost, but not quite, slamming his office door. "Okay, Donna, I know you need to talk to him," said Yves quietly, "I can finish the tables. Go on ahead."

"You sure?" I asked, but then I looked at him and said, "Thanks, Yves," because he had a look on his face that said, *get going*. I left, putting my dishrag in the sink, and almost flew down the hall to Father Douglas' office. "Father Douglas?" I called, opening his office door, and then said, "Oops, sorry, should I have knocked?"

He looked a little startled, but managed to smile at me and said, "That's all right, what is it?"

I came in and walked in front of his desk, and then I couldn't hold back anymore, starting to cry. "Hey," he said gently, "why don't you sit down? This must be important."

I pulled up one of the wooden chairs he kept in the room for visitors, and I tried to stop crying. I found a used tissue in my pocket and tried to wipe my face. "Here," said Father Douglas, "I have these on my desk right here, you can always have some," and pushed over a box of tissues.

"Thanks, Father Douglas," I said, once I got my breath, and wiped my face again.

Then I looked at him. "I saw Rick last night, over by the park. He was going to sleep in the park, probably on some bench somewhere. I guess that's what he must have done. I hate that whole idea, but he wouldn't come here. He told me why he left. That man Dave, who came from Dayton just like Rick did, is the man who raped him. Remember when I told you that Rick was raped, in the State hospital? I guess it is his private business, but I am so angry at that Dave, I just want to scream at him."

"Well, don't do that, or at least, not in here. I wonder if the police could do something about this."

"I just don't know if Rick would go to the police," I sighed, "I don't think so. He says he won't, that the police won't listen to him. Anyway, who knows where he is right now? I'm so angry, I can't even look at Dave."

"Well, now," said Father Douglas, "Dave still lives here, you know, and we don't know for sure that this is true. Rick isn't always reliable. And, now, listen," he could see that I was about to argue, "we are all fond of Rick, but we have to remember. This is his battle, not really ours. We can support him, but we can't fight it for him. It's up to him to do something about it."

I just stared at Father Douglas. His battle? That didn't sound right to me. It certainly wasn't a fair fight. He was a victim, not a fighter. Still, I wasn't sure how to argue this with Father Douglas. Bottom line, he was my boss. "Okay, well, I'll try to control myself when Dave's around. It won't be easy."

"Remember, part of this job is maintaining some emotional distance from the men. That's important, even though I appreciate your concern for Rick."

I looked at him. He was giving me one of his patient, but firm, looks. Then he said, gently, "I hope he comes back, too. Let's pray for him and see."

"Okay, Father Douglas," I said, bowing my head, and left. I decided to try it. Wandering over to the Chapel, I ducked in, expecting the usual, calm peaceful scene. I heard voices. In the far-left corner of the room, not so far from the altar, I saw Dave and two of those men that followed him around. And I was enraged to find that I was smelling cigarettes. What were they doing? I walked toward the front. "Excuse me," I said, "but you're not really supposed to be talking in here, and you definitely can't smoke in here."

"We just wanted a quiet place where we can talk. What's it to you?" asked Dave, defiantly.

"We have the TV room for that, or you can take it outside. Now you guys need to leave, or else I can get Father Douglas."

They skulked past me, Dave giving me a sullen glare. Once they shut the door, I walked straight up to the altar, knelt in front of it, and tried to pray. My brain was on fire with rage at Dave, and John Smith, and the man who was menacing Penny at the hospital, back years ago. All people who raped and molested and menaced! I was furious and wanted to rid the world of them. I began sobbing, gently, as the anger passed through my body like a wave. I wished I was home, where I could sit at my window with a can of Tab and a cigarette again, but that wouldn't make the anger stop. I prayed, "Lord, please help me see what to do about this. I want to help Rick, but I don't know how. Please help me, and Rick, and Penny, and her mother and everybody that this has happened to."

I finally wiped my face and got up. It would be time to help with lunch pretty soon. I wondered if I could tell Yves about this. He was a kind man, and I thought I could trust him to keep Rick's story to himself. "Yves," I said, as I went in the kitchen, "I can't quite believe what Father Douglas said, wait until I tell you."

But he was standing over a large pot, stirring, and he looked like he needed help. "Thank God you're back," he said, "quick, stir this while I get the tomato soup started. I knew I should have put the mac and cheese in the oven. I'm using the stovetop to save some time, you know? But it might have been a mistake. It has some really good cheese in it, but please don't let it burn, okay? Father Douglas got the donation from some restaurant. The men will love it. Oh, I'm sorry, Donna, I guess I didn't hear what you said. Are you okay?"

"Sure," I said, since Yves clearly didn't have time for the whole story, "okay, I'll stir the mac and cheese. It smells great. I hope there will be some left over for me."

Just then, one of the men popped his head in and asked if he could get coffee. I said sure, and he came in and got some, balancing three cups and saucers on the way out. I suddenly realized this was one of the guys I'd seen with Dave earlier in the chapel. I followed him out and there were the three of them again, sitting at one of the tables.

I walked over to them, not really knowing what I wanted to say but knowing I had to say something. I went up to their table and looked straight at Dave. "It may interest you to know that I saw Rick in town last night. Turns out he remembers you very well from Dayton."

Dave just gave me a sullen glare, and said, "So? Not your business, lady."

His two friends slunk away, putting the saucers over their cups, to take them to the TV room, probably. "So, you are lucky we did not go straight to the police."

He made a noise that was sort of a snarl crossed with a guffaw. "I don't think Rick's going to any police any time soon," he said, "but if he does, they'll probably just lock him up, loony tunes that he is."

I'm not sure why, but I found myself looking intently at his eyes as he talked. He really did have at least five pupils, of varying sizes but mostly small, in one eye, and three in the other. "I'm not so sure about that. And I am pretty sure that I am gonna find out," I finished, nearly exhaling fire.

"Sure," he said with a snicker, "you go find out, then. Keep yourself busy. You can't do nothing to me."

Then he turned back to his coffee, and I stomped back to the kitchen, muttering, "Oh yeah, well maybe I can't do nothing, but I'm pretty sure I can do something."

When I got back to the kitchen, Yves was sweating over both pots at once, and whined, "Young lady, why did you leave my nice pot of macaroni to burn like this."

I just collapsed in a chair and stared at him. Tears came to my eyes, but I blinked them back, took a deep breath, and said, "Aw, Yves, I'm sorry. I hope it's not ruined."

He said, "Oh, I don't think it's that bad yet. You get over here and stir for me, all right? I'm going to add some more butter to loosen it up. But don't go away again, okay? You all right?" he looked at me, suddenly concerned.

"Yeah, I'm okay," I said, and just stirred the macaroni, wondering if I could last the whole day with that Dave hanging around.

I was thinking of going home after we served lunch, but one thing led to another and somehow, I didn't see much of Dave. Probably he was avoiding me, which was fine. Finally, I got a little time to myself, and I asked Father Douglas if I could use the phone to call a friend of mine. He smiled and said, "Sure, in fact you can take it into the other room if you want."

I smiled and thanked him, and then I did exactly that. Somewhere in my pocketbook, I was pretty sure, was the number of that policeman I was talking to at Miranda's funeral. Some man answered the phone, and I realized it might be the police station at Possumtown. Did Possumtown have two policemen? I found that surprising, somehow. "Hi," I said, "can I talk to Ed?"

He said, "Sure."

I heard him as he was handing the phone over saying, "Some woman on the phone. You got a girl-friend, Ed?"

Ed got on the phone; "Hi, who is this?"

"This is Donna. I hope you remember, I was talking with you at Miranda's funeral, about her kids and all."

"Sure, I remember," he said, "of course. You were friends with Miranda, and now you live in Pittsburgh."

"That's right," I said, "I wanted to ask you about something."

I told him about Rick, and how Dave showed up. "Is there anything any of us can do about this? Rick doesn't think the police here would help him. I can't believe that."

"Well," he said, "I actually worked in Pittsburgh, just for a few years, after my training. It's a long time ago, now, I guess almost sixteen or seventeen years since I came here to Possumtown. But I'm still in touch with a couple of the guys out there. Tell you what, I just have a few things to do tomorrow morn-ing. How about if I come out there in the afternoon just to see what's going on? It'll only take a few hours for me to get out there, I should be there around one o'clock."

"I hate to put you to all that trouble," I said, amazed that he was willing to drive all that way.

"It's all right," he said, "I don't mind driving, and it might be a good idea for me to show up if I want to talk to any police up there in Pittsburgh, rather than just calling on the phone. You say this man Dave is still there at your House?"

"Yes, and he gives every indication of staying there, too."

"That's fine. You might want to keep your distance from him till I get a chance to get out there and take a look at him. Don't say anything to him that might make him think of leaving."

"Okay, I get it. Don't worry. This is so nice of you and such a relief to be getting your help. I guess I'll see you tomorrow, then."

I put down the phone feeling like the world was a different place. "Wow, thank you, God," I said, breathing out a long sigh.

I took the phone in to Father Douglas, and said, "Thanks, Father, and if you don't have anything else, I think I'll go spend some time in the Chapel."

He smiled and said, "That sounds great."

I walked down the hall, feeling like I was floating, so great was my sense of relief. I walked into the little chapel, leaving the lights off, and walked straight up to the altar and bowed. Then, just because I felt like it, I walked around the altar toward the crucifix. I glanced back, seeing no one in the chapel, and noticing the little shelf behind the altar with a pair of reading glasses, a flashlight, and Father Douglas' notebook again. I would have to bring it to him later. I sat down before the crucifix and drew my knees up, resting my head on them, and stayed like that until I smelled cooking and knew it was time to help with dinner.

CHAPTER SEVENTEEN

A Strange Sandwich

THE NEXT DAY WAS such a peaceful day to begin with. We made meatloaf for dinner the night before, and there was leftover meatloaf for sandwiches for lunch. It seemed an auspicious time for Rick to show up since he loved Yves' meatloaf, saying it was even better than his mother's. Yves even joked, later on, that maybe Rick smelled the meatloaf from the park. He certainly was hungry when he showed up, and dirty and tired, with none of that money I gave him.

"I can't sleep in the park anymore," he moaned in Father Douglas' office. "Some group of kids were chasing me around the park all last night. I didn't think I was ever going to lose them, but some nice stranger yelled at them and got them to go away. He said I could stay at his house, but I told him no, so I found another bench, but I didn't really sleep from being scared that something else would happen. I lost some of that money you gave me, so I couldn't take a bus. But at least I had dinner last night, and I bought some cigarettes, so thanks for that."

"Well, I'm so sorry," I said, "but I'm glad you're here. It's not safe for you to be sleeping outside in the park."

"We've been talking about that," said Father Douglas, "could you go to the kitchen and get him some food? He doesn't want to take the chance of running into Dave, and that's probably for the best, for now."

I said, "Sure," and got up to go.

"Rick," said Father Douglas, "can you eat in the waiting room, is that okay?"

Rick agreed, and went to the waiting area, probably eager for meatloaf. Father Douglas held up his hand for me to wait as I made to leave. "What is it, Father?" I asked him.

"I was talking with Rick about going to the police. He was so anxious, as soon as I mentioned it. It's not going to be easy to get him to do that. Maybe best not to discuss it with him, for now."

"Okay, Father, I understand," I said.

I didn't want to make Rick any more anxious than he was already, that was for sure. I went to the kitchen and told Yves I needed a sandwich for Rick, and he made one with a huge slice of meat loaf and lots of ketchup. I ran back to the waiting room with that, and a big mug of hot coffee, and Rick commenced to eating with gusto. I just sat, half watching and half just wondering what to say. I really wanted him to go to the police, but I also knew that Father Douglas was right about that. I honestly wasn't sure what I could say that wouldn't make him anxious. Eventually I said, "I'm sorry for what you went through, Rick. I bet having a nice full stomach will help, though."

"I just don't want to run into that man again," he said with his mouth full, his voice almost hysterical, "and I don't know what to do about it. I just can't go to the police. I just can't," he shook his head at me, woefully.

"I remember," I said, "you told me that the other day. I get that it's hard. Tell you what, when you're done eating, maybe we can sneak over to the chapel, real quick. Being there might calm you, and it's one place where we are unlikely to run into Dave."

"Mmpf," he uttered, and wolfed down some more sandwich. In minutes he was done, and shifted his attention to the coffee, gulping it gratefully, if rather noisily.

"Okay," he said finally, "that sounds all right. That is one place where I might be able to calm down and think, you're right about that. Hey, know what, I wrote another poem. I wrote it while I was just sitting quietly in the park the other day. I can read it to you."

"Great," I said, chuckling, "so if you're done, let's go. We'll be quiet, okay?"

I figured Dave would still be in the cafeteria, sitting with his little group of unhappy followers over coffee, but I didn't want to take any chances. And for once, Rick was quiet, even walking quietly instead of his usual shuffle. And it was so quiet and calm in the chapel. Sometimes you could hear little bits of sound from the TV room down the hall, but that was muf-fled by some drapes that had been thoughtfully placed along the back wall. We didn't turn the lights on, since the place was dimly lit by the small stained-glass windows, high up in the west-facing left wall.

We went along to the front, sitting on the left side, looking up at the altar and the crucifix. "I love that carving of the crucifix," I said, "when you look at that face, it really seems like He could understand just about anything you might be going through. Such a look of suffering mixed with understanding and kindness."

"Yes," said Rick, "I've noticed that. It must've been a talented man who made that carving. Any idea who it was?"

"You'd have to ask Father Douglas," I said, smil-ing, "he probably knows. He's been here a long time."

"Do you know when he started here?"

"I'm not sure. Maybe about ten years ago, more or less."

"He's a great guy. I don't know how I would've managed in Pittsburgh without this place. Course, I don't know if I can really stay here, now."

Suddenly right behind us was Dave's voice, saying with his usual sarcastic snicker, "Don't worry about it, friend, I can solve that problem for you."

Rick jumped out of the pew and ran behind the altar, but Dave was right behind him. "Lookit this," shouted Dave, pulling something out of his pocket that looked like an old bike chain, "remember this, Rick? Remember how I put it around your hands, back in Dayton? I bet you do," his eyes gleaming tri-umphantly as he backed Rick up to the crucifix. "Tell you what, you like this old cross so much? I'm gonna chain you up to it and set it on fire, how you gonna like that?"

Rick was whimpering and trying to leap and wriggle away from Dave, but Dave was too strong to let go. I dashed up behind them, remembering about the flashlight, and made to hit Dave over the head with it, but he ducked and grabbed my hand. "You wanna help, huh? That's all right, I'll chain you both up and watch you burn."

He got out a lighter, lit it and held it toward me with one hand while he held Rick with the other. I fell backward, but managed to grab the flashlight again and made to hit him with it. At the same time, I turned it on by accident and it shone right in Dave's face. It was brighter than I would have expected, and he screamed and stumbled backward, dropping the lighter and chain, holding his hands in front of his eyes. I realized at once that his many-pupiled eyes must be sensitive to light. As he fell, Rick wrested out of his grasp and managed to jump on him with both feet at once. I grabbed the chain up and yelled, "You hold him down, Rick, and I'll tie him with his own chain," and started to wrap the chain around his chest and arms.

"Yes," shouted Rick, who pinned Dave's arms down with his knees. I managed to get the chain around his arms and was tying it with a square knot, thank you Girl Scouts. But just as I was finishing the knot, Dave reared up his shoulders and bucked Rick off of him, screaming with rage. I tried to push him back down, but he got up and rushed at me, backing me up to the crucifix and ramming me so hard I saw stars, and the crucifix fell down behind me. I thought I was going to die, but I noticed Rick sort of darting up next to us and pulling up the crucifix from behind me, swinging it around and slamming it against the back of Dave's head. He fell against me and I wriggled away, getting loose and yelling, "Run!" to Rick as we both went as fast as we could to the exit of the chapel.

Of course, Dave got up in no time and was after us, running with his arms still tethered close to his body. We sped down the hallway of the house, Yves shouting behind us and running after, and Father Douglas nearly getting run down as he poked his head out to see who was making the noise. We careened out the door, Dave right behind us when Rick turned around and slammed the door against him, but he couldn't get it shut and Dave burst out after us, as we dashed into the road, not looking whether any cars were coming.

Wouldn't you know, it was Penny coming down the road toward us in her mother's station wagon, her eyes wide with fear when she saw us run out into the road in front of her, but swiftly changing to anger when she saw Dave. She must've put her foot on the gas to make sure to hit him, because she got him just as he made it to the middle of the road, and pinned him against another car that had just turned the corner, making a very tight Dave sandwich. Dave was still raging, unable to move his legs but bellowing and shaking his fists at Penny and us as we panted on the sidewalk, looking back at him in amazement.

The other car, as luck would have it, was a police car, and at the wheel was Ed. He leaped out of the car, went swiftly over to Dave and gave him his Miranda rights over Dave's screaming, somehow putting cuffs on his wildly waving arms. They kept the cars like that until the ambulance got there, just to make sure he couldn't go anywhere, and in fact nothing was broken, just a few bad bruises, I would guess. I was thanking Ed, when Rick came up and peered over my shoulder, asking, "Where are they taking Dave?"

Ed answered that Dave would be going to a locked unit at the hospital and released straight into police custody. "So, you won't be letting him go? That's good," said Rick, looking exhausted.

Ed wanted to talk to Father Douglas, but he turned to Rick and said, "I really need to take a statement from you, but I have to ask Father Douglas a few questions first. You'll wait right here?"

"Sure," said Rick, and I said I would wait with him. Penny came up to us and said, "Wow, I really hope we're seeing the last of that guy Dave. Thank God he won't be hanging around the House to scare us anymore."

Penny and I talked for a few minutes, and then Ed came back. "Where's Rick?" he asked me, and I said, "He's right there. Oh, no he isn't. Oh for crying out loud, I'm so sorry Ed. I don't see him anywhere. He must have made a run for it while I was talking to Penny. I only turned my back for a minute, I can't believe it."

"Well, never mind," said Ed with a laugh, "I guess I do have that effect on some people."

••• CHAPTER EIGHTEEN •••
The Poet Returns

"THAT RICK," I SAID to Ed, "he's quite the escape artist. He did that a couple of days ago, I just turned around to do something else for minute and whoops, he's gone."

Ed laughed and I started to laugh too, but then stopped and said, "Ouch, you know what, it kind of hurts to laugh all of a sudden."

"Uh-oh," said Ed, "did you get hurt?"

"Dave pushed me up against the crucifix, in the House, when he attacked us. I'm lucky Rick managed to pick up the crucifix and hit him with it, otherwise I might be dead."

Ed laughed again, a bit sadly, and said, "Good thinking on Rick's part. Sounds like you might have a broken rib or two."

Then Father Douglas came up and said, "Thanks so much, officer. How did you happen to be here at just the right time?"

We explained about how we'd met at the funeral, and the phone call, and Father Douglas listened carefully, and said, "So Donna asked for your help, and you came just at the right time. I am so grateful, and especially since you drove so far to be here to help, Ed."

"Hey, this is my job," said Ed, "I'm grateful myself, that we got here in time to help Donna, and now we have this guy Dave in custody. I can get the Pittsburgh police to hold him just on the strength of what happened here, but I'm guessing there will be other reasons to hold him once we check out his prints, whether we get to talk to Rick or not."

I was just trying to breathe without hurting, and when two ambulances pulled up, they got Dave out from between the cars and strapped him to a gurney, still screaming, and wheeled him into an ambulance, which carried him away. They helped me into the other ambulance, and took me to that same ER in Pittsburgh where I used to work. It turned out that two of my right ribs were broken, but there wasn't much to be done for treatment except to wait for them to heal.

When they discharged me from the hospital, I was going to get a cab home, but decided to get out at my local store to get some ice cream, for sure, this time. When I got out of the store, I walked home along the park again, since it was cooler near the trees. And when I came up to the bench where I'd spoken with Rick only the night before last, there he was again. In spite of the heat, he was shaking.

I sat down next to him, and he looked at me through those glasses of his. "I'd offer you some ice cream, but you look cold," I said.

"I think I ran almost all the way here," he said, mournfully. "I'm so tired. You have anything in that bag besides ice cream? Some cold cuts or something?"

"You mean like meatloaf?" I said with a smile, "come back to the store with me and I'll get you a sandwich."

So, we walked there, and he waited outside while I got him a turkey and cheese sub with mayo and mustard, and a nice cold Coke. As he was eating and slurping, I tried to start a conversation. "Look," I said, "Ed called me at the hospital, right before they discharged me. He's at the police station. He's pretty sure he can get them to hold Dave for a while, but it would be so much easier to do that if he got to talk to you. Just think how much better you'd feel, knowing that Dave was paying for what he did. And as soon as we're done, I'll get a cab to take us back to the House. You don't want to sleep out here, after what happened today."

He was finishing the sandwich with record speed. "Listen," he said, "thanks for the sandwich. But I have to get going. I can't go to the police station, no way, no way."

He started walking, and I followed him. "Well," I said, "we're going in the right direction, let's just walk over there. I'll go in and see if I can find Ed, and he can come out and talk to you. You don't have to go in."

It took a few hours of following him around to get him anywhere near the police station. This isn't a great thing to be doing with broken ribs, and many times I had to sit down for a few minutes to catch my breath. He could easily have run off again, but somehow, he didn't. Once we were close to the police station, I left him sitting on a bench near a streetlight, and went in to look for Ed. I had no faith at all that Rick would still be waiting by the same streetlight when we came back. But he was. I guess he really didn't want to spend the night in the park. It was kind of unusual to take a statement this way, but Ed said they'd agreed to let Rick stay outside. Ed wrote it all down patiently on a clipboard as we sat on the bench together under that streetlight. It was a warm night, so it was actually kind of pleasant, sitting there. Then Rick and I set out to find a cab to take us back to the House. Ed offered to take us in a squad car, but Rick looked like he would take off running at the very suggestion, so I said no thanks.

We found a cab as we walked toward the river, lucky for us because by that time, it was the middle of the night. When we got back, Yves had gone home, of course, but I made some coffee, and we found part of a cherry pie in the fridge. We enjoyed Yves' cherry pie with our coffee, and talked about the day, leaving out the really awful parts. "Good thing you were waiting for me at that streetlight," I said.

"What happened to the ice cream?" Rick wanted to know.

"Oh, it melted. I threw it away at the police station. No big deal," I said, adding, "I was worried you would take off while I was getting Ed. I'm glad you didn't."

"I was worried you couldn't find Ed," he said. "I don't think I could've said all that to some other cop. He's all right, kind of."

"Anyway, does it feel good to be back here, now?" I asked him.

"Yeah," he said, "I'll be all right. I'll walk you to your car and have a cigarette."

"Where'd you get the cigarettes from? Old Gold Filters, wow, those are strong, aren't they?"

"I bought them with that money you gave me. Lucky thing that Dave didn't smash them all. Want one?"

I almost took one, then I said, "Nah, I got some Virginia Slims in my bag. I'll smoke in the car on the way home."

Once we were outside, he lit a cigarette with a match, inhaled it and said, "My mom loves doing that, by the way, smoking in the car."

"How does she like England? Did you hear from them?"

"They don't know where I am. I have an address for them. When I get a chance, I'll write."

"She's smoking British cigarettes now," I giggled, "wonder how she likes them."

"Probably beats these. Well, who cares? You know, this place does feel better now. Like Dylan said in that song, 'It's not a house, it's a home.'"

"That's great," I said, and opened my car door, waiting to see him walk back in before I left.

"Hey, cheerio," I added, as he opened the door to the House, "isn't that what they say over there?"

He just kind of snorted at me, his glasses flashing in the moonlight, walked in, and closed the door behind him.

CHAPTER NINETEEN

Lunch at the Diner

THE FOLLOWING WEEKEND, I went home for a visit, and that Saturday around lunchtime, I went over to the Possumtown police station. I barely got my head in the door before the lady in back who did the typing called out, "Hey, I think that's Ed's Donna. Honey, don't I know you from church?" and she came trotting over, wearing a housecoat over pajamas and slippers.

"Wow," I said, "you look comfortable. I gotta talk to them where I work, about coming to work like this. Great idea."

"Hey," she said, "All's I do is sit back there and type, so who cares. How're your parents, Donna? I heard your Dad was having arthritis."

Meanwhile the policeman behind the desk went over to a door and yelled, "Hey Ed, your girlfriend's here," and Ed came running out, looking embarrassed and said to him quietly, "Hey shut up, you know I don't have a girlfriend."

The policeman said, "Sure," sarcastically and made a knowing face behind Ed's back to the typing lady, who started laughing.

Ed ran up to me, grabbed my arm and said, "Excuse me, dear," to the lady as he rushed me outside.

"A little too much in there sometimes," he commented with an embarrassed smile, "I think we have a bit too much time on our hands lately. Course, you gotta hope it stays that way. You wanna go to the diner?"

I looked at him. He was smiling so kindly, I began to wish this was more than just a friendly get together. But all I said was, "Where else?" and we walked a few blocks up the road to the little neighborhood diner.

This was really all Possumtown had in the way of restaurants, apart from the A&W and the picnic tables in back of the store, by the ball fields. We sat in one of the booths and ordered coffee. The owner knew both of us, but he needed to talk with Ed about something, and I didn't really listen, checking out the specials on the menu. The chili looked good. Finally, the owner left us, and we got to talk. We kept our voices down, and there were only a few other people there, sitting at the counter, so we had enough privacy to work with.

After some small talk, he leaned in and gave me that smile again. *Uh-oh*, I thought, *I bet this is going to be a tricky question.* "So, I meant to ask you," he said, "you were saying you had some kind of history with John Smith? I guess anybody who went to school with him might have been affected by that behavior problem of his."

"Well, I guess I might have been in the category of 'most affected.' I might as well tell you, I made the mistake of getting in a car with him after he'd been drinking and he, well, I hate to go into detail . . . ." My face probably told him the story.

"Oh, wow, don't worry, I get it. That's awful. You know, that wouldn't have been in any way your fault. The guy is a sociopath, sort of a human predator. It might be partly from things that happened to him, but, hey, that's how he is, whatever the reason. Did you ever talk to anybody about it?"

"Only my sister and my friend, Denise. And then recently, since I've been working at the Catholic Worker House, I had a few, like, counseling sessions with Father Douglas about it. He actually suggested that I should try to pray for John Smith. He said it was for me, so I could get over being angry about it. I sort of get that, but I find it really hard to do."

"That's some suggestion, but I guess I see what he means, you know? I try to think of John, and other guys like him that I deal with, like that, sometimes. I mean, I try to imagine what they might have been like when they were really young and innocent, and how their parents might have tried to help them. Or in John's case, how they might have abused him."

"You know, it's really something, but I found myself wondering about that guy Dave, watching him caught there between those cars, yelling and screaming. I couldn't help wondering how he got like that, and how his family feels about it."

"Of course, I wouldn't know about Dave, but John's parents were pretty abusive. It's possible that he had behavior issues to begin with that got them frustrated, so they overdid it with the punishment, but anyway, they were way out of line with that."

"You know, that is really terrible. I never knew that. I guess nobody deserves that from their parents."

"Oh, yeah. He said they actually had a cat of nine tails, a kind of an old-fashioned whip, like they used in the bad old days. It's hard to imagine anyone using a thing like that on a child. But I believe him. There are parents who use whips on their kids around here, even now. A few, anyway, that I know of. It's disturbing."

"It sure is. I wouldn't be able to talk to someone like that. I really don't think I could do your job."

"Well," he said, chuckling, "it's not like your job is easy. It was great, how you got that guy Rick to give us a statement. I can't believe you dragged him all the way from the park to the police station, with broken ribs. You must have been exhausted."

"Oh, boy," I said, "exhausted is not the word. I'm wondering how long it'll be before I can laugh without it hurting."

"Sorry to hear that. I was hoping you'd be okay by now," he said with a look of concern.

"Oh, I'm okay," I said, smiling, "It's not as bad as it was. Another week or two and I'll probably forget all about it. Anyway, I can get around and do what I need to do. I wouldn't be here in Possumtown if I couldn't."

Ed smiled and asked, "How's Rick doing, anyway?"

"He's okay, thank God. And thank you for helping with him. That was some situation. He told me he couldn't have said all that to a different cop."

I was thinking about John again. "You know," I went on, "when I ran into you the first time, at the A&W, that was not long after John did that to me. I left school early and didn't go home because of something that happened when I ran into him at school."

"He was teasing you about it?"

"Worse than that. He found me and my friend Denise out in the ball field and threatened to do it to her."

"What did you do?"

"I kicked him in the you-know-what's, and he fell over and threw up. Denise told me to run, and I did."

Ed laughed so hard I thought his coffee might come out his nose. When he recovered, he said, "That's great. I can just imagine it. And that's when you wound up at the A&W?"

"Yeah. I was so scared. I kept thinking John would be looking for me in his car, but he didn't. And you know what? He never bothered me about it, and last time I saw him, at the fifth high-school reunion, he didn't even look at me. I was glad he didn't."

"He didn't want people to know that a girl did that to him. Anyway, he may have sort of blocked it out of his mind, you know? People do that sometimes."

"Huh," I said, "well, it's fine with me if he did. But that forgiveness idea bothers me. I mean, what he did had such a big effect on my life, really. Please don't repeat that, though. I don't normally talk about it that much." Suddenly, I got a wave of panic, thinking, *Why did I say all this to someone I don't really know that well? Especially a guy that, well, maybe, I'm beginning to like.*

"Listen," he said, "I hear all kinds of things in this line of work, and I'm good at keeping things to myself. I would never repeat your story to anyone. But I'm glad you're talking to Father Douglas. Those experiences can do a lot of damage, but with the right help, you can get better. He sounds like he has some good ideas. He didn't expect you to go and forgive John right away, did he?"

"No, he said to take my time," I said, "and you're right, I do think I'm lucky to have his help."

"He sounds good to me. Hey, maybe I should come out there and talk to him myself."

"Well, you'd be welcome to come any time, I'm sure. We're all so grateful to have Rick back," I said, and then leaned back and looked at him for a minute. I knew I didn't really have the nerve to ask him out, but I didn't know when I would see him again, so I figured I had to say something. Finally, I said, quietly, "I mean, maybe he could help you work out why a guy as nice as you doesn't have a girlfriend."

He looked at me, wide-eyed with surprise. Then he looked down, his face getting red. *Damn,* I was thinking, *I said the wrong thing. This comes from being out of practice. I mean let's face it, I've never had any practice at this. He's probably going to leave, now.*

"Well," he said finally, and then looked up at me, with a very guarded expression, "you know, I do wonder about that myself sometimes. Hey, if you think he could help me with that, it would certainly be worth a shot. Of course, it's just possible that I may wind up needing some help from you with that, too."

His face got even redder after he said that, but he still looked at me. I looked back, speechless for once, and then started to breathe again. "Uh," I said, "well, sure, anything to help you, officer Ed," giving him my best shot at a flirtacious smile and wondering what on earth that even looked like.

He laughed, and took my hand. He looked at me again and said, "So you wouldn't mind if I gave you a call sometime?"

"Not at all," I said, smiling again and feeling like a bunch of butterflies just took off somewhere in my chest. I looked down for a second, hoping my hand wasn't sweaty. But when I looked up, he was still smiling. Finally, I was able to say, "So why don't you come over to the House sometime? We'd all be so glad to see you, and then maybe we could think of somewhere to go for dinner. That'll give you a chance to get acquainted with Pittsburgh again, I'm sure it must've changed a lot since your training days."

"I'd love that," he said, "plus it would maybe give me a chance to talk to Father Douglas, if he has time. That could work out just great."

"Yes, it would be great," I agreed, beaming, "just let me know when you're coming so we can fix up a really nice lunch, and I'll show you around."

Epilogue

Less than a week later, Ed did come to Pittsburgh to visit. He really liked Yves, and after we all had some coffee together in the kitchen, I took Ed to the office to meet Father Douglas. When I introduced them, I couldn't help kidding Ed, saying, "I have to ask you, Father Douglas, could you make some time to give Ed one of your little talks? He seems like he could really use your help."

Ed laughed and Father Douglas said, a bit stiffly but looking pleased, "Well, of course. My dear, any policeman is likely to have a lot on his mind."

And so, it was arranged that Ed would come back, every few weeks or so, depending on his work schedule, to help out a little and have one of those little talks with Father Douglas. "And," Ed said to me later, "this'll give me time to get reacquainted with Pittsburgh."

He laughed when I looked annoyed. "And you, of course, Miss Donna. That's my real reason for coming out here, if you must know. Besides giving folks at the station something to talk about," and he gave me a smile, while he was saying this, that I was happy to see.

"By the way," I asked him, "did you hear anything about that guy Dave?"

"The one I almost ran over with the car? Lucky for me, your friend Penny was coming along from the other side and we got him like that. Made it look like a clever way of catching a suspect, instead of carelessly knocking people down with a police car, which could have got me in a lot of trouble. You know, his parents came and brought a lawyer, and got him into a locked ward in a state hospital in Ohio. Better for him than jail, but he isn't likely to get out for a really long time. Your friend Rick has nothing to worry about."

"All the same," I said thoughtfully, "unless he asks, I think I'll keep that information to myself. I am pretty sure Rick would worry anyway. I hope you are right."

My friend Denise kept going to her meetings, and I would still go with her sometimes, when I was out in Possumtown, visiting not just my family and her, but Ed too, now. But truthfully, I was relieved when the day came that she told me, she didn't need me to come anymore. "Now," she said, "I do want you to be there for my anniversary, God willing that I stay sober that long. I mean, you helped me get started with this, and I'm really grateful. But for the other meetings, it's better if you don't come. I finally realized that I'm not really supposed to be bringing you. Most meetings are just for alcoholics."

"Well," I said, "fine with me. And now, I wonder if you would come somewhere with me. I decided that I want to go visit John Smith in jail."

"What?" she asked in disbelief, and it took me a while to explain about what I was working on with Father Douglas. But she seemed to finally get it, saying, "You know, that sounds a little like what people say about working the Steps. Sure, I'll drive you there. It's kind of far, all the way to that jail in Reading. Can I bring Jeff?"

"Sure, of course you can bring your son. We can make it a family trip. I can sit with him in the car while you visit John, if you want to do that."

She looked at me, almost laughing, and said, "Um, no, Donna, I don't want to visit John. I'll just drive you up there, and then we'll all get something to eat. Okay?"

So that's what we did, on a warm weekend in early September, and it was a good day. John didn't have much to say, but he seemed pleased to hear that I forgave him. He claimed he didn't remember that night, but he also said he was sorry if he had hurt me. I suppose that was better than nothing. He was interested to hear that Denise was going to meetings, and said that he was trying them himself, in jail. He complained about the food, and I said I would look into sending him something.

The trip back seemed to go quickly. Although the visit went as well as I could have hoped, I was happier when I knew we were getting close to home, and Denise and Jeff seemed happier, too. "Hey," said Denise, "You know there's only one place we can go for lunch," and Jeff said, "Of course, the cold-custard stand, yay."

The cold-custard stand, with its ages-old neon sign, was at a location in town near one of the ramps to the turnpike, and it was a favorite of just about everyone I knew. Their chili dogs were the best. As we sat at the picnic table with our chili dogs and Cokes, I thought about John, and Miranda, and how even the worst of our past together could begin to seem like part of a larger plan. I thought about Ed too, and said a quick prayer concerning the future and him. And there in the warm September sunlight, it felt like the best day ever.

Acknowledgments

I would like to thank Tom Bird and his employees, Donna Velasco, Arnel Ollete, and Janelle Kutz, without whose guidance this book would not exist. I also wish to thank, for their needed and much appreciated help in editing, Idony Lisle and Bill Worth, who made suggestions that really brought the book to life. And again, with love and gratitude, Susan Bowen, for her helpful suggestions and artistic feedback about the cover, and Myles Paulson, for his specific encouragement during various phases in which I was considering giving up on the book altogether. Most of all, I would like to dedicate this book to people struggling with mental illness everywhere, in the hope that there may be more answers, in future, to make their lives more livable.

About the Author

This is Dorothy North's second book. She lives in New York with several cats and dogs, including Snaggy, whose photo was taken in 2016 by the author's sister, Lucinda Giles.